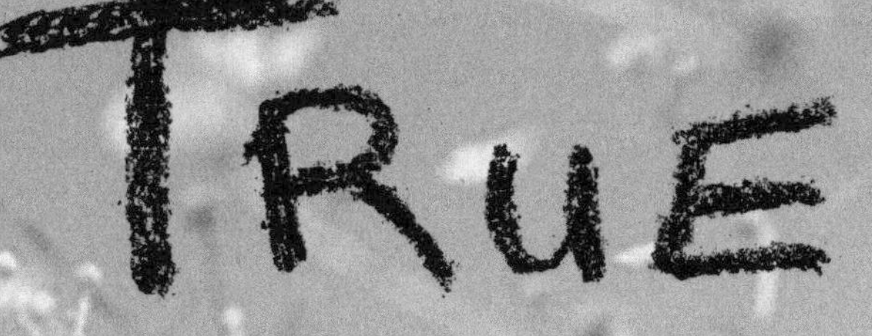

Praise for

Katherine Hannigan's

debut novel, *Ida B . . .*

and Her Plans to Maximize Fun,

Avoid Disaster, and (Possibly) Save the World

ALA *Booklist* Editors' Choice

BookSense #1 Children's Pick

Publishers Weekly Best Book

New York Times Bestseller

Nominated for 29 state awards

"This is exactly the kind of book I want to read."

—Kate DiCamillo, winner of the Newbery Medal for *The Tale of Despereaux*

"I can't wait for everyone to read it and meet Ida B . . ."

—Brian Selznick, winner of the Caldecott Medal for *The Invention of Hugo Cabret*

"With just the right amount of tension in the plot, a spot-on grasp of human emotions, and Ida B's delightful turns of phrase, this book begs to be read aloud."

—*School Library Journal* (starred review)

"Hannigan shows remarkable understanding of a stubborn child's perspective in her honest, poignant portrayal of loss and rebirth."

—*Publishers Weekly* (starred review)

"A poignant, affirming, and often funny debut."

—*Kirkus Reviews* (starred review)

"Full of spunk and imagination, debut author Katherine Hannigan's *Ida B* bursts onto the kid-lit scene like a Ramona Quimby for the new millennium."

—*Time Out New York Kids*

Katherine Hannigan

...SORT OF

THESE ARE UNCORRECTED ADVANCE PROOFS.
Please check any quotations or attributions against the bound copy of this book. We urge this for the sake of editorial accuracy as well as for your legal protection and ours.

Greenwillow Books
An Imprint of HarperCollins*Publishers*

 Printed in the United States of America. For information address HarperCollins Children's Books, a division of HarperCollins Publishers, 10 East 53rd Street, New York, NY 10022.

www.harpercollinschildrens.com

The text of this book is set in Perpetua.

Book design by Sylvie Le Floc'h

Library of Congress Cataloging-in-Publication Data

Hannigan, Katherine.

True / by Katherine Hannigan.

p. cm.

"Greenwillow Books."

Summary: For most of her eleven years, Delly has been in trouble without knowing why, until her little brother, R.B., and a strange, silent new friend, Ferris, help her find a way to be good—and happy—again.

ISBN 978-0-06-196873-0 (trade bdg.) — ISBN 978-0-06-196874-7 (lib. bdg.)

[1. Behavior—Fiction. 2. Selective mutism—Fiction. 3. Friendship—Fiction. 4. Brothers and sisters—Fiction. 5. Family life—Fiction. 6. Schools—Fiction. 7. Self-control—Fiction.] I. Title.

PZ7.H19816Del 2011 [Fic]—dc22 2010017315

11 12 13 14 15 TK 10 9 8 7 6 5 4 3 2 1

First Edition

Greenwillow Books

For the children who don't speak.
And for those who hear them anyway,
and make a safe place

Chapter 1

Delly Pattison was tiny. Her hair curled tight to her head, like a copper halo. Her voice was raspy, as if a load of gravel lined her throat.

And Delly Pattison was trouBLE: little trouble on the way to BIG TROUBLE, and getting closer to it every day.

Delly's trouble wasn't mean. It always started with her thinking something would be fun and good. It always ended with somebody yelling, "Delaware Pattison, to your room!" or, "Welcome to detention, Ms. Pattison. Again." And there Delly'd be, wondering how something that had seemed so right could go so, so wrong.

Truth is, trouble didn't find Delly till she was six years old—the summer the Pattisons went to the County Fair.

Clarice Pattison'd said to Boomer, "Let's take the kids. They can look at the cows, and go on a couple of rides."

"Sounds good," Boomer agreed.

So they piled all those children—Dallas, the oldest, then Tallahassee, Montana, Galveston, Delaware, and RB, the baby—into the van and headed out.

There were eight Pattisons in the parking lot. Boomer checked again when they entered the Poultry Pavilion. It wasn't till they got to the Cattle Corral that Clarice realized somebody'd gone missing. She counted heads and then she shouted, "Delly!"

There was no reply.

The Pattisons scattered, searching under tractors and behind hay bales for her.

By then, though, Delly'd had ten minutes of solitude in the Poultry Pavilion.

Clayton Fitch saw it first: Chickens of every sort, strutting out the front door of the building like they were going on vacation.

"The chickens are loose," he squeaked. Then he ran in circles, squealing, "Great God A'mighty, the chickens are loose!"

Officer Verena Tibbetts was at the main gate, making sure nobody got in for free. She came tearing over, hollering, "Clayton, quit squawking and catch those chickens!" She charged into the Pavilion, searching for the cause of the chaos.

Halfway down the line of cages, she found it. There was Delly Pattison, standing on a crate. She had her hand in a coop, pushing a chicken's backside. "Go on now. You're free," she rasped as it flapped to the floor.

Officer Tibbetts ran at her. She picked Delly up, and held her so close they could smell each other. "It is bad to let the chickens out of their cages! BAD, BAD, BAD!" she roared. Then she braced herself for the bawling that was sure to follow.

But this is what Delly did instead: She smiled.

The ends of her mouth went up, almost to her eyeballs. "You're funny." She giggled.

At first, Verena was so surprised she just stared. Then she growled.

And that's how Clarice found them, one growling and the other grinning.

"Take this child home," Officer Tibbetts told her.

So she did.

It took ten people two hours to get those chickens back in their cages. When they were done, Delly was Number One on Verena Tibbetts's list of The Worst Children in River Bluffs.

Chapter 2

The trouble went on from there.

When she was seven, Delly lifted a pan of brownies off Mabel Silcox's back porch.

"Where did these come from?" Clarice asked, when she found them half-eaten in Delly's room.

"Ms. Silcox left me a surpresent," Delly told her. Her smile was so big it squeezed her eyes shut.

"What's a surpresent?" Clarice inquired.

"It's a present that's a surprise. It's the best kind," Delly explained.

Mabel Silcox had another word for it. "I've been robbed!" she hollered.

Clarice brought Delly in for questioning. "You

still want to call those brownies a present?"

"A surpresent, Ma," she corrected her.

"To your room," Clarice commanded.

"But—," she argued.

"Go," Clarice replied.

So she did.

"Sometimes Ma is a mysturiosity," she told the empty brownie pan.

When she was eight, Delly decided it was too fine a day outside to spend it inside and at school. "A holiDelly," she declared it.

Before she took off, though, she wrote a note that read, Please excuse Delly. She'll be back tomorrow. She signed it, and sent it in to school with the Dettbarn twins. She didn't want anybody worrying.

So she did not fret, swinging and sliding at the park, when Officer Tibbetts pulled up in her cruiser. She was not worried when the policewoman ordered, "Delly, get in the car." From the backseat, she waved at the people they passed, like she was in a holiDelly parade.

She was confused, though, when Clarice and Boomer told her, "You're grounded, for a week."

"This is a disaster," she told them.

They did not disagree.

When she was nine, Delly found the canoe Clayton Fitch left by the river, and took it for a ride. She wanted to see where she'd end up.

"We're going on a Dellyventure," she told the boat, and it rocked and rolled down the river for her.

They came aground in Hickory Corners, two towns and ten miles away. The police called Clarice.

In the van going home, Clarice's lips were sealed tight with worry and fury.

So Delly filled the silence. "Ma, I saw turtles as big as boulders," she said.

"That boat banged into rocks and went backwards, but I wasn't scared," she went on.

"Ma, next time I'm going all the way to—,"

Clarice pulled the van off the road. "Delly," she yelled, "nobody knew where you were. You could have been killed!" Her whole body was shaking.

"But Ma," she explained, like Clarice was a little kid, "I was wearing a life jacket."

"Enough!" Clarice shouted, and they were moving again.

Back home, Delly did find out where she'd end up if she took a canoe down the river: "In your room, for two weeks," Clarice told her.

She had to pay Clayton Fitch a rental fee, too. "Bad, badder, baddest," he said as she set the money in his hand.

When she was ten, Delly invented the Nocussictionary.

She made up words people could say instead of swearing, like "Shikes", "Chizzle" and "Bawlgrammit." She wrote them down, then she shared them with all the kids she knew. "Not cussing," she told them. "Can't be trouble."

There was something about the way the children said those words, though, so loud and with such delight, that made the grownups suspicious.

They asked questions, and "The Nocussictionary" and "Delly" were the answers to all of them.

For three dinners, Delly had soap for dessert.

Bubbles floated out of her mouth as she complained, "But Ma, we weren't swearing."

"That's not the point," Clarice answered.

"What is?" she gurgled.

Clarice just shook her head.

There was more: Big trouble, small trouble, Christmas and birthday trouble, too.

Still, eating soap or stuck in her room, Delly never quit believing that fun was just two steps and a "Bawlgrammit" away. And she didn't stop smiling.

Chapter 3

Maybe it was because she was tiny, or because her hair curled too tightly to her head. Or maybe it was from being called "Bad" so many times.

Whatever it was, when Delly was eleven she took a turn. And it wasn't for the better.

At first it was small things: She quit doing homework, and started talking out of turn.

None of that was new, exactly. Delly'd always forget homework for some fun, and she wasn't much for manners.

But now, when her teacher, Lionel Terwilliger, told her, "Ms. Pattison, please wait. Someone else is speaking," she didn't smile and say, "Sorry," like before. She slumped down in her seat. When he said, "Your homework is late. You may bring it tomorrow, with a penalty," instead of saying, "Okay, thanks," she mumbled, "Just give me the zero."

"I'm worried about Delly," Clarice told Boomer.

He nodded. "The bad grades."

"That's not it," she said.

"All those trips with Officer Tibbetts?"

"It's her smile." Clarice's voice cracked. "It's gone."

The smile that filled Delly's face had disappeared. In its place was a smirk. The smirk pinched her mouth crooked, and just pretended happiness. It hurt Clarice's heart every time she saw it.

"She'll get it back," Boomer assured her.

Clarice nodded, hoping that was true.

Delly did get something, but it wasn't her smile. She got the fight, instead.

It happened on a Wednesday at recess. Alice Mae Gunderman kicked her ball up on the school roof, and Alice Mae cried.

Delly saw the whole thing. She knew what to do for Alice Mae and for fun.

She shimmied up the downspout and onto the roof. "Hey, Alice Mae," she hollered, and kicked the ball back to her.

Delly knew she'd done good. The corners of her mouth started to curl.

Then Ms. Niederbaum, the recess monitor, spotted her. "Delly Pattison, get off that roof!" she shouted.

So she did.

There was a big map of the United States on the basketball court. Alaska was way off by itself. It was for time outs.

"To Alaska," Ms. Niederbaum commanded.

Delly looked at Alice Mae, smiling and playing again. "But—" she muttered.

"Go," Ms. Niederbaum ordered.

And Delly didn't ask, "Why?" because she knew the answer: She was bad, she was wrong, she was trouble.

She trudged to the State of Solitary Confinement, hearing those words, "bad, wrong, trouble," over and over, as if they were her name.

Danny Novello saw the whole thing, too. He was grinning.

He ran up beside Delly, bringing a crowd of kids with him. "She's small enough," he told them. "And she climbs like one. Let's see if she can talk."

"Can...you...speak?" he asked the side of her face.

The crowd giggled.

"Do...you...talk?" he shouted in her ear.

Now, any other day, Delly would have hit him with a, "Hey, Nobraino, talk to me when you get one," and that would have shut him down. But the only words she could think of were "bad, wrong, trouble", and they were about her. "Grrrr," she growled.

"Can't talk. Must be a monkey!" Novello yelled.

The laughs buzzed around Delly, stinging her.

She slumped down on Alaska. "Bad, wrong, trouble," pounded her with every heartbeat. She could feel the tears pooling up behind her eyeballs.

But Delly Pattison didn't cry. So she said something mad, to stop the sad. "I'm sick of feeling bad," she grumbled.

Right away, her eyes quit watering.

"I'm sick of getting in trouble and not knowing why." She slapped the state beneath her.

Her heart stopped hurting.

The mad was taking over. It felt better than being sad.

The feeling bad wasn't done with her, though. "So what are you going to do about it?" it sneered.

The mad didn't know.

Till Novello walked by, teasing, "Hey monkey, time to go back to the zoo."

It took Delly nine seconds to catch Novello and fling him to the ground. It was six seconds of twisting his nose till he screamed, "I take it back! I take it back!"

It took Ms. Niederbaum just two seconds to yank Delly off him. She got 9,000 seconds of sitting on Alaska for that.

But for those fifteen seconds of fight, Delly

wasn't sad and she didn't feel bad. And for once, she understood why she was in trouble. It was worth it.

After that, if somebody snickered behind her, Delly shoved him. If a child whispered anywhere near her, Delly took her down. She got into so many fights with so many kids, only RB and the Dettbarn twins would come close. Every other friend deserted her.

One day, after two calls from school and a Special Dellylivery from Officer Tibbetts, Clarice had had enough. "What is going on with you, Delly?" she yelled. "What is wrong?"

So Delly told her, no smirk or smart stuff, "I'm horribadible, Ma."

"What's horribadible?" Clarice asked.

"Horrible, terrible bad," Delly told her, "like everybody says."

"That's not true," Clarice replied. "You're not bad."

But Clarice hadn't changed Delly's mind about her badness. Not one bit.

Chapter 4

Delly Pattison was born smiling.

"That's one happy baby," Mabel Silcox said.

"That baby's too happy," Clayton Fitch scowled.

Even after the trouble took over, Delly started every day with a smile. As soon as her eyes opened she'd cheer, "Jiminy fipes!" and run down to breakfast grinning.

But now, the feeling bad went to bed with her. "Another day of trouble," it would tell her when she woke up. She'd wait till Clarice hollered, "Last call, Delly!" to drag herself out of bed. It'd been a long time since her smile made it downstairs.

The Saturday the Boyds came to town, though,

was different. That morning, the top of Delly's head twitched, like every hair was hopping with excitement. Then her whole body tingled.

It was the feeling that told her a surpresent was coming.

"Happy Hallelujah," she shouted, and bounced out of bed.

The surpresent feeling didn't show up too often; maybe once or twice a year. But every time it did, something wonderful came Delly's way, like the hockey skates she got out of Teeters's garbage, or the five dollars she found on the IGA floor. All Delly had to do was show up at the right place at the right time, and a surpresent would be waiting for her.

That morning, the surpresent feeling filled her, so there was no room for feeling bad. Her lips couldn't help curling at the corners.

She ran to the top of the stairs. "Ma," she called.

Clarice came to the bottom of the steps, with a spatula in her hand.

"Are you baking a cake?" she asked

"No," Clarice told her.

"Did you get us a puppy?"

"No."

"Are we going on a trip?"

"Delly." Clarice was waving the spatula like a weapon. "You get down here, or you'll be on a trip to I Missed My Breakfast Land."

"Okay, Ma." She grinned, not minding Clarice's tone or temper. Because after all the trouble, something good was finally coming to her.

When she got downstairs, the smile was still there.

Clarice Pattison worked at the hardware store in town. Boomer Pattison drove truck, so he was gone more than he was home. That left Clarice alone with six children, one of them Delly. She was a hard-working woman, tired most of the time.

Four of the Pattison children were peaceful. But Galveston and Delly were like volatile chemicals—put near each other, those girls would explode.

Mealtimes were worst for it: Food had been thrown, children had flown.

So Clarice assigned seats. She set Galveston beside her, and put Delly between Dallas and Tallahassee. If a fight broke out, Clarice could grab Gal, and those two would squeeze Delly till she calmed down.

That morning, though, Galveston got after Delly the second she stepped in the kitchen. "We're almost done fixing breakfast," she hissed. "You're supposed to make toast. Get going."

Any other day, Delly would have grabbed the spatula. "Gal, I'm going to flip you like a giant pancake." Next thing, the fur would have been flying.

But Delly had so much surpresent feeling in her, there was no room for the fight. She walked to the toaster, humming.

"What's wrong with her?" Galveston jeered.

Nobody answered, because nobody knew.

At the table, Delly smiled at her orange juice, then hummed through her pancakes.

Clarice ate with one hand on Galveston, holding tight to the peace.

When she was done eating, Delly said sweetly, "Hey, anybody hear about something special happening today?"

The others were stunned by the sweetness. "What sort of something special?" Clarice asked.

"Like free candy at the IGA. Or Karlson's dog having puppies."

"I haven't heard anything," Clarice told her. "Why?"

Delly's eyes got big and she whispered, as if saying it might scare it away, "It's a surpresent, Ma. A surpresent's coming, and I can't miss it."

Galveston snickered, "Here we go—," and Clarice's claw squeezed her silent.

Now, Clarice Pattison liked surpresents about as much as she liked seeing Officer Tibbetts at her door: More often than not, they meant trouble. But Delly had smiled. And she was looking at Clarice, her eyes full of needing something good. "You'll find it," she told her.

Delly grinned so all her teeth showed. As soon as she set her plate in the sink, she ran to the door, calling, "I'm going."

"Delaware Pattison!" Clarice yelled.

And the smile Clarice had waited months to see was wiped away. "What?" Delly muttered, ready to hear what she'd done wrong.

So instead of saying, "I don't want the police near this neighborhood," Clarice told her, "Take a coat."

That quick, the smile was back. "It's going to be gimungous, Ma," she said, and grabbed her jacket.

At the door, she whispered to the world, "Here I come, surpresent. Smack me down with yourself."

Chapter 5

RB Pattison was seven years old, and he loved Delly like Christmas.

Dellyventures were his favorite. He liked it best if she invited him, but he'd tag along if she forgot.

Delly was running, her feet whap, whapping the concrete. She was concentrating so hard on her surpresent, she didn't hear the whap, whapping of somebody else's feet behind her.

Till she got to the end of the street. She turned to see who the whapper was.

And RB ran right into her.

"What the glub are you doing?" she demanded.

"Going with you." He grinned.

"No, RB," she told him. "Now go home."

RB stood still, like a possum pretending.

Delly turned and started walking again, whap, whap.

Two seconds later, there was that other whapping.

Delly faced him. "RB," she hollered, "I'm trying to find my surpresent."

"I know," he answered.

"That means no lugdraggerers tagging along."

"What's a lugdraggerer?" he asked.

"It's somebody who slows you down, and has to tie his shoe fifty times a day."

"I'm not a lugdraggerer," he told her.

And he was so sure of it, she couldn't tell him otherwise.

"Please, Del?" he said sweetly.

"Bawlgrammit," she grumbled, because she couldn't say "No" to that.

"You got to do what I tell you," she ordered.

"I know."

"No whining."

"I know."

"No messing around."

"I know, I know, I know."

"And what about food for you? I'm not going home till I find my surpresent."

"I got food in here. For both of us." He showed her his backpack. It was loaded. Delly just hoped it wasn't cans of sardines and broken up crackers like last time.

"You're something," she told him.

But he heard it in her voice; he was something good.

She took off again, with him beside her. At Main Street, RB grabbed her hand.

"Just for crossing," she said.

"I know."

She didn't shake him off, though, when they got to the other side.

Chapter 6

They walked all over town, seeking the surpresent.

They went to the river and looked for packages, wrapped or unwrapped, floating down it. They checked the garbage cans at the nicest houses in town. But there was no surpresent tingle; not even a twitch.

Delly sent RB to knock on Mabel Silcox's door. "You baking something today, Ms. Silcox?" he inquired.

She wasn't.

They stopped at the Dettbarn twins's. Julius and Sissy were sitting on the stoop with a shoebox between them.

"What you got?" Delly asked.

They showed her the mouse their cat brought home, still alive. They'd put it in the box with a washcloth for a blanket and some peanut butter to eat.

"You want it?" they asked Delly.

She thought about the fun she could have with that mouse and Galveston. She closed her eyes and waited for the tingle to tell her this was her surpresent. It didn't come.

"No, but thanks," she answered.

RB and Delly sat on the steps of St. Eunice's church, with their hands folded and their eyes raised to heaven for ten whole minutes, but nothing happened.

"This is a mysturiosity." Delly sighed.

They ate lunch at the church. RB had stuck a jar of grape jelly and a loaf of bread in his backpack.

"Knife?" Delly asked.

He shook his head.

"Water?"

He shrugged.

So they ate giant-hunks-of-jelly-on-bread sandwiches. Their teeth and tongues turned slimy purple with white chunks.

"Where are we going now?" RB asked when they were done.

"Let's go to the IGA," she decided.

The corner in front of the IGA was the busiest spot in town. If something special came to River Bluffs, it was sure to pass that place. They parked themselves on the sidewalk by the front door and waited.

But it was boring, just sitting there. Delly got an idea to pass the time. "I'm going to teach you how to spit," she told him.

"Yay." RB clapped.

"Watch," she said. She hacked up a goober, and sent it flying down the sidewalk. It landed with a SPLAT. It was purple, with white chunks in it.

"Wow," RB said.

"Now you do it," she directed.

He puckered up and moved his mouth back and

forth. Delly gazed down the walk, watching for the splatter.

Instead, she heard a "t-t-t" beside her. She felt a mist of spit on her face.

"Hey!" she shouted. "Not t-t-t. Not through your teeth. Like this." She hacked up another one. Thup it left her lips, then splat. "Your mouth's a spitzooka," she told him.

RB nodded. He got a giant goober on his tongue. And his mouth exploded.

It was big and purple. It went more up than out. But it landed with a whap, sending saliva in every direction.

"Nice," Delly said, and RB glowed.

Then it was spit fireworks at the IGA. Those two were so busy perfecting their spit skills, they didn't notice people trying to get by without getting splattered.

Clayton Fitch turned them in. "You got those little Pattisons outside, spitting purple at everybody," he tattled to Norma the cashier.

Norma looked out the window and two purple

spitballs sailed by. And there was Mabel Silcox, all eighty years of her, trying to jump out of their way.

"Delly," Norma scowled. She ran to the window and banged on it.

Delly was too busy to hear her.

Norma was yelling now, things like "calling the police" and "jail time." She was so loud RB heard her through the glass.

"Delly," he told his sister, "you'd better look."

So she did.

But by then Norma was shooting out the door of the IGA, like she'd been blasted out of a bazooka herself. "Delly Pattison," she shouted, "I'm taking you to Verena!"

Delly heard that. "RB," she yelled. "Run!"

The three of them raced down the walk, with Norma howling, "Stop those Pattisons!"

When suddenly, the air was filled with a strange song. It was metal squeaking and something creaking, rubber thumping, and something else bumping. It was coming straight at them.

They all stopped running and turned to it.

That's when Delly got the tingle, bigger and stronger than ever.

"My surpresent," she breathed.

Chapter 7

Five minutes before, the green Impala with the trailer behind it had turned off the highway onto River Bluffs Road.

The car's brakes squeaked every time they got tapped. One wheel whump, whumped as it went around. Wind got into the trailer and made a wailing whistle as it passed through.

On their own, each of those sounds might rub an ear raw. But together, they made a song, a sad song of things gone wrong and barely hanging on.

The green Impala with the trailer behind it squeaked and whumped into town. It passed the Dettbarns, yelling, "Mouse for sale!" and silenced them with the song. It screeched by the park, and the kids on the basketball court quit playing. Finally, the green Impala with the trailer behind it squealed toward the stop by the IGA.

By the time Delly saw it, she was tingling to her toes. It was the surpresent coming at her so loud she couldn't miss it.

She forgot about Norma. She walked to the curb and waited. "I was worried," she whispered, "but you're here."

She closed her eyes. "Better than ten pans of brownies," she told herself. "Better than a new sister to replace Galveston." She could tell by the tingle.

She felt the heat of the car beside her. She opened her eyes and gazed into the green Impala.

"It's...,"she exclaimed, as she searched the front seat. "It's...," she said, scanning the back.

Then she muttered, "What the glub?"

The back of the car was empty. Up front, a man was driving. And in the seat next to Delly was a boy, a pale, skinny one with short hair. He was hunched over, wearing a too-big t-shirt.

"It's nothing?" she mumbled.

The tingling was so strong, though, it was shaking her. "You got to be here somewhere," she insisted.

She searched again.

But there was nothing close to a surpresent in that car. There was nothing that said, "See, Delly? After all the trouble, here's something good. There's still hope for you."

She felt her hope leaving her. "No," she rasped.

The "No" joined the rumble of the car so no one heard it.

Except the boy. He glanced over at her.

After, Delly only remembered his eyes. They were blue like ice, with sad stories frozen inside. They made her shiver.

The boy turned away. Then the green Impala with the trailer behind it whumped and whistled through the stop, over the bridge, and out the River Road.

Delly stood at the curb, blinking. Every time she closed her eyes, she saw the boy's blue ones.

"Delly." RB tugged on her.

"Huh."

"You ready to go? 'Cause here comes Norma."

With the song gone, Norma was blasting off again. "You stay right there!" she shouted.

"Run!" Delly yelled.

They sprinted full-speed, no-stops all the way home. They dashed to Delly's room and dove behind the bed.

"Del?" RB asked, still gulping air.

"Huh."

"Was that your surpresent?"

It took her a second to answer. "No," she told him. Then she hollered so the world would know it, "That was not my surpresent!"

Chapter 8

The old Hennepin place was on the River Road, just outside of town.

The house was gray, with a gray drive and gray stoop. A basketball hoop hung on the gray garage. Woods surrounded the yard, so even when the sun shone, the house stayed in shadow.

The green Impala with the trailer behind it squeaked to a stop in the drive. The driver's door creaked open and whumped shut. Squawk then thump went the passenger's side.

The man opened up the house. Ferris Boyd opened the trailer. They carried their things inside, without a word between them.

The birds were talking, though. They were everywhere, chirping and chattering like the Welcome Wagon on wings.

It was almost dusk when they were done. The man went into the house, and a light came on in the back of it.

Ferris Boyd reached into the trunk of the green Impala. She pulled out a backpack and an old basketball. She shuffled up the drive.

As she got to the steps, there was a tiny rustle, a sound so small nobody'd notice.

Ferris Boyd stopped. She tilted her right ear toward it.

There was a crackle.

Slowly, Ferris Boyd turned. Her eyes traveled along bushes and between trees, till she found the one who'd called her. It sat in the shadows at the edge of the woods. Its eyes glowed golden.

Ferris Boyd blinked.

The eyes blinked back. "Mahowrrrr?" it wondered.

And Ferris Boyd answered, without saying a word.

It flicked its tail twice, All right.

The girl went into the house. In a minute, she was on the stoop again. She set a bowl in the grass. She sat on the steps and waited.

As the creature crept across the lawn, the girl stayed still. When it put its head in the bowl, she didn't move.

When it was finished, it walked past her, bumping her shins with its body. Ferris Boyd raised one hand, so her fingers brushed its back, and it purred.

It ran across the lawn, and stopped at the edge of the brush. The tail flicked twice, Good night.

Ferris Boyd nodded.

Then the black cat disappeared in the darkness.

The pale, skinny girl slipped into the house. A light came on in the upstairs window.

Chapter 9

At dinner, Delly was still thinking about her surpresent. But now, there was no smiling. Now, instead of hoping for a puppy, or a magic wand to make Galveston disappear, she was wondering, Was the tingle just teasing me? And worse, Will anything good ever happen to me again?

It felt bad, the kind of bad she'd need a fight to forget.

Clarice was occupied with other things. It wasn't that she forgot about the surpresent, but with Montana dogging her, "Ma, I need money for my date," and Tallahassee begging, "Can I stay at Fern Teeter's, pleeeease?" there was no room to remember.

"Ma, we need more beans," RB announced.

While Clarice was up filling the bowl, Galveston quit chewing her potatoes to chew on Delly. "So," she sniped, "where's that surpresent? Is it in the garage? Or does Verena have it locked up?"

The other children held their breath. Dallas and Tallahassee got ready to squeeze.

But Delly stared at her plate, like she hadn't heard a word.

The others sighed and went back to their food.

And Delly was flying across the table. She was gone before Dallas and Tallahassee could touch her.

She landed on Galveston's chest, and got her by the hair. She was yanking it left, then right, like it was the reins on a bucking bronco.

Gal was making strange sounds, "Wooo-ooo-ooo," and Delly was yelling, "That's so funny, Gal. How come you're not laughing now?"

Clarice got to them first. "Let go!" she hollered as she pried off the tiny, terrible fingers.

Galveston was clutching her scalp, screaming, "Am I bald? Did she bald me?"

Dallas threw Delly over his shoulder, and started up the stairs. "GAL-VES-TOOON!" she howled.

"You stay in your room till I tell you!" Clarice shouted after her.

"Rowr rowr rowr," Delly growled.

"But Ma," Gal cried, "she has dishes."

In a flash, Clarice was in her face. "You'll do dishes tonight," she fumed. "And you'll do them every night for a week."

Gal thought about whining some more, but Clarice was too close. "Yes, Ma," she whimpered.

Clarice was waiting till she calmed down to talk to Delly. That didn't happen till two hours later.

Delly was on her bed, facing the wall, when her mom walked in the room.

"Don't leave this house till Monday morning," Clarice ordered. "And you've got dishes next week. With your sister." She turned to go.

"Ma," the rasp called.

"What is it?" Clarice said, still hard.

"It didn't come."

"What didn't come?" she asked.

And the rasp was so filled with sadness, it almost couldn't speak. "My surpresent."

Then Clarice remembered. "Oh," she sighed. She sat on the edge of Delly's bed. She watched the tiny back breathing. "I thought you were going to meet it," she said, softly.

"I did."

"Well, where'd you go?" she wondered.

Delly told her all the places she'd searched for the surpresent.

"There's your problem," Clarice said. "That surpresent couldn't catch you, moving around like that."

Clarice's words sent little sparks of hope to Delly's heart. She turned toward her mom. "You think?"

"Yep. You got to stay in one place. Which is good, because tomorrow you're grounded."

But Delly needed more than that to get her hope back. "Ma, are you sure?"

And Clarice, remembering Delly's smile that morning, said, "Sure."

That did it. Hope flickered in Delly's heart, then it went to full-flame. She lay there in the warmth of Clarice's "Sure."

"Good night, Delly," Clarice said as she got up off the bed.

"Good night, Ma," the rasp replied, because now it was.

Chapter 10

Brud Kinney lived out the River Road, about a half mile past the old Hennepin place. He was in the fifth grade at St. Stanislaus, the boys' school two towns away.

Brud Kinney loved basketball. He played before the bus picked him up; he played at night with the porch light shining. He played all day, in his head, while his teachers talked.

And on Sundays, he was at the park, playing with the other River Bluffs kids. He played till his arms ached and his fingertips rubbed raw.

Because what Brud Kinney wanted most was to play basketball like nothing nobody'd ever seen, only better.

Brud's two front teeth were fake. They glowed white in the light. He got those teeth making a basket, so they were like tooth-shaped trophies.

They'd been playing at the park: Brud, Gwennie, Tater, the Dettbarns, and Novello. It was a close game, and it was getting mean.

Tater got the ball in to Gwennie. "Brud," she hollered, and hurled it down the court.

With Novello breathing down his back, Brud grabbed it. He took a step, and jumped high in the air. His hands sent the ball soaring into the sky.

As he came back to earth, Brud's eyes watched and his ears listened for the swish of the score.

So he didn't see Novello's elbow coming at him. He didn't hear Gwennie shout, "Watch out!" He hardly felt the bone hammer his mouth.

Brud's body hit the ground with a thud. His mouth started shooting blood, like a crimson geyser.

Danny Novello was dancing around the court, screaming, "There are teeth in my arm! His teeth are in my elbow!"

Tater and Gwennie leaned over Brud.

"Wow," was all Tater could say.

"You all right?" Gwennie asked him.

But Brud only wanted to know, "Did I m-m-make the sh-sh-sh-shot?"

"Yep," she told him.

Then Brud passed out, smiling.

Chapter 11

Sunday morning, early, Brud was heading into town to practice.

In real life, he had his basketball under one arm, and he was riding his bike down the River Road.

But in his head, Brud wasn't on a bike at all. In his head, he was already at the park, playing ball. He was shooting from the inside, the outside, and every shot was a swish. In his head, Brud was playing like nothing nobody'd ever seen, only better.

And today, Brud didn't just see it in his head; he was hearing it, too. There was the ping, ping, ping of a ball bouncing, the clang of it against the rim. For the first time ever, Brud's vision had a soundtrack.

By the time he got to the bridge, though, the pings and clangs had almost disappeared. "H-h-hey," he said, like somebody'd messed with his movie. He stopped his bike.

But the pings and clangs kept coming. From behind him.

So Brud rode back out the River Road. The sounds got louder as he came to the old Hennepin place.

He set his bike and ball in the ditch. And between trees, he saw it.

At the end of the drive was a boy, a pale, skinny one. He had short hair like Brud's. He wore a "Lakers" shirt, like the one Brud had at home. And he was running, dribbling a ball between his legs and behind his back like it was nothing. Then he jumped, and sent the ball to the hoop. Swish, it made the sound of perfection.

It was Brud's vision. Without Brud.

Now some people, seeing somebody steal their vision, might get mad. Not Brud Kinney. Maybe if I watch this boy, he thought, I could learn to play like that, too. That got him so excited, his mouth whistled, "Whewwwweee."

The whistle stopped the boy.

Brud slapped his hands over his mouth. "Sh-sh-shoot," he mumbled, and ducked behind the brush.

The boy held the ball tight to him. His scared eyes searched along the bushes.

Now some people, after almost getting caught, might hightail it out of there. Or they might say, "Hey, I was watching you. Want to play?"

Not Brud. He loved basketball too much to leave. And he didn't want to ruin it with trying to talk. "Don't s-s-s-stop," he whispered.

Finally, the boy got back to playing.

"Yes," he breathed.

But that wasn't enough for Brud. I need to get closer, he thought.

So he snuck, behind trees and bushes, till he was across from the boy. He peeked between branches. Don't mess me up again, his head told his mouth, and he watched.

Up close, the boy was even better. He could

dribble backward, forward, and zigzagging. He could shoot from inside, outside, and everywhere in between.

Brud was taking it in. In his head, he talked to himself like a teacher: Look how he holds the ball. Look how low he goes before he jumps. His head was so busy teaching, it didn't notice what the rest of him was up to.

Because Brud's body was already trying it out. When the boy dribbled down the drive, Brud's hands pushed an invisible ball. When the boy crouched with the ball over his head, Brud's knees bent. And when the boy sprang into the air, Brud did, too.

He came crashing through the bushes with his arms over his head. He landed in front of the boy.

They stared at each other for a second. The boy's eyes were filled with fear. He turned, ready to run.

Brud knew what to do. He had to tell the boy, fast, "Hey, I'm Brud. I was just watching you play. You're good."

As the boy sprinted to the stoop, Brud took a

deep breath. "H-hey," he hollered, "I'm B-B-B-B-"

Now the boy was at the door

Please work, just this once, Brud begged his mouth.

His jaw jerked. His lips opened wide. Then he yelled, "Hey, I'm B-B-B-!"

The door slammed. The boy was gone.

Now some people, after scaring somebody like that, might go to the door and explain things. But at the door, Brud'd still be saying, "B-B-B-."

And some people, Brud's head said, after seeing a stranger jump out of the bushes, might CALL THE POLICE.

"Sh-shoot," he stammered, and sped down the drive.

As Brud rode into River Bluffs, his head cussed his mouth: You're always messing me up. You wrecked it, and there's nothing to show for it.

But he was wrong about that.

Because when Brud got to the park and started playing, he was better. He could feel it in the way he dribbled the ball. He could see it, the way the ball went to the basket.

"You're playing real good today, Brud," Gwennie told him.

He didn't try to say, "Th-th-thanks."

Danny Novello watched him, squinty-eyed suspicious. "Think you're going pro or something?" he sneered.

Brud just shrugged.

That night, Brud Kinney lay in bed with the moon shining in his window. He thought about the boy, dribbling and jumping and shooting like that. He thought about playing at the park, and how sweet the swish of the net sounded.

Then Brud Kinney smiled. The two teeth twinkled in the moonlight, like stars.

Chapter 12

Delly spent Sunday on the front porch, staying in one spot like Clarice had suggested.

She sat on the steps, spinning her head so she wouldn't miss anything. All the while her mouth was mumbling, "Come on, come on, come on..." even when she ate her meals.

After lunch, RB sat down beside her. "What are you doing?"

"Waiting...come on...for my surpresent... come on," she answered.

RB thought for a minute. "Are you grounded for fighting with Gal?"

With her head going round and round, it was

hard to tell if she was nodding. "Del?"

She stopped for a second. "We moved around too much yesterday," she explained. "I'm staying here so the surpresent can find me."

"Oh." RB watched her head twirl for a while, but it wasn't any fun. "I'm going," he told her.

Without Delly, though, there wasn't much to do. He threw rocks at the side of the house till Clarice yelled, "Who's hitting my house?" He was picking up worms with a stick when the idea came to him. "I'll bring it to her," he breathed.

"Delly, is this your surpresent?" he said as he stuck a half-eaten candy bar in her face.

Delly waited for the tingle to tell. "Nope," she told him, and went back to mumbling.

After a while, he returned. "Is this it?" It was Tallahassee's trick quarter.

"No," she sighed.

He found it under the back porch. He covered it with a cloth, and carried it to her. "Delly, Delly, Delly!" He was bouncing on the step and singing.

Her head quit swinging.

"What about this?" He pulled the cloth away, and there it was: A squirrel carcass. There was no fur on it, just dark skin stretched over bones, with the tail still sticking out.

Delly sucked in air so she whistled. "A bawlgram squirrel mummy," she whispered. She touched the skin with her finger.

"Well, is it? Is it? Is it?" RB grinned.

Delly closed her eyes and wished for the tingle, because that squirrel was as good as any surpresent got. She waited and waited, but nothing happened. When she opened her eyes, she didn't say anything.

RB covered it up again. "I'll save it for you," he said.

"You go play with Cletis," she rasped. Because it hurt, watching him lose his hope, too.

"You sure?" he asked.

Her head whirled.

All the way to Cletis's, RB chanted, "Come on, come on, come on."

It was dark when Clarice came to get her. "Delly, time for bed," she called.

"Come on... Can't... come on," she replied. If she got up, the hope would go for good.

Clarice sat beside her. "Delly," she said softly, "I know you want a surpresent. But you don't need one. You got good all around you." She put her hands out like she was holding it for her.

Delly shook her head hard, because she knew about the good all around her. She needed to know there was good in her. She needed something in the world to say, "Delly Pattison, you're not just trouble. Here's a surpresent to prove it."

"Ma. I'm..." She tried to tell her, but there wasn't a word for feeling so sad and close to hopeless. "Tired," she sighed, and got up off the step.

"Good night, Delly," Clarice told her.

"Night," she said, because that's all it was.

Chapter 13

That night, Delly didn't get a surpresent. Sleep brought her something, though, because in the morning she came downstairs with a smirk.

Walking to school, RB asked her, "You okay?"

"Oh yeah," she sneered, "because I got good all around me.

"Who needs a surpresent with all this good around me?" she went on, kicking the sidewalk. "No more waiting and hoping for me, RB. I'm going to grab the good around me." She swiped the air.

RB just watched her.

At the school entrance, Delly held the door. "Go on," she told him.

So he did.

When he got to his classroom, RB turned to tell his sister, "See ya."

But there was no sister to be seen. "No," he gasped, and headed for the door.

Till Ms. Niederbaum nabbed him. "Your room's this way," she said, and steered him back.

From his desk, RB stared out the window. "Oh, Delly," he whispered.

Weekday mornings, Norma at the IGA made doughnuts. She made vanilla-glazed with nuts, maple-glazed with coconut, chocolate with chocolate icing and chocolate sprinkles. Those days, the air around the IGA smelled so good you'd want to eat it.

Delly peeked to make sure Norma wasn't at the checkout, then headed straight for the doughnut case. "Mm-mmm," she greeted them. She grabbed a sack, and filled it with a dozen Dellylicious delights.

Vern Teeter rang her up at the register. "You having a party?"

"Something like that." Delly smirked.

"Better hurry," he warned her, "or you'll be late for school."

"Oh, I will," she promised.

She ran out of the IGA, and raced to the river. It wasn't two minutes till she was sitting under the River Road bridge, deciding which doughnut to devour first. "Triple chocolate," she decided.

"Ma's right," she said as she snatched it out of the sack. "I don't need a surpresent. I got a Dellypresent." With Dellypresents, there'd be no more waiting, no worrying if she was good enough. "Perfecterrific," she proclaimed.

With the river rolling by and the sun shining on her, she raised the doughnut in the air. "Good all around me." She grinned, and took a bite. "Good in me, too," she declared, spitting chocolate chunks.

Clayton Fitch was on his way to the IGA when Delly'd dashed by him. It wasn't a minute till he was on the phone to Officer Tibbetts.

"Verena," he squawked, "that Pattison's running to the riv—"

Officer Tibbetts hung up before he could finish. Delly wouldn't be celebrating alone.

It wasn't three minutes till the policewoman had parked the cruiser by the bridge. There was half a doughnut hanging out of Delly's mouth when she ordered, "Drop it, Delaware."

"What the glub?" Delly muttered, and the doughnut plopped to the ground.

Officer Tibbetts seized the bag. "You won't need these where you're going." She grabbed the girl's arm.

Delly was too stunned to struggle.

The policewoman led her to the cruiser. She put her in back, behind the bars.

"But it was perfecterrific," Delly mumbled, as they drove to school with the siren screaming.

Chapter 14

Lionel Terwilliger taught the fifth grade, including Delly. He liked big words, and he called everybody "Ms." or "Mr."

What Delly liked about Lionel Terwilliger, though, was he never shamed her. When she was in trouble, he'd bend down beside her and whisper, "Ms. Pattison, there is an issue we need to discuss." Then he'd tell her what she'd done wrong. Delly always listened; somehow, she always messed up again. Still, she was never just trouble to Lionel Terwilliger.

So when Ms. Niederbaum brought Delly to the classroom and told him, "Delaware's joining us after all," he said, "Ms. Pattison, your presence is always appreciated."

Delly was still in shock. She stared at the floor, seeing river and rocks instead.

"We have a new student," he told her. "Since you missed introductions, I will present you now."

Lionel Terwilliger put his hand on Delly's shoulder, and that made her look up. He raised his arm, and Delly's eyes followed it.

To a boy. The bawlgram no surpresent boy.

"Ms. Delaware Pattison," he announced, "this is Ms. Ferris Boyd."

Delly didn't say it to be mean. She said it because, after being wrong about everything else, she was right about this.

"That's no Ms.," she announced. "That's a boy."

Right away, there were giggles. Danny Novello laughed out loud. Bright red ran up the boy's neck and covered his face.

"This is Ms. Boyd," Lionel Terwilliger insisted.

"But he—"

"Ms. Pattison," he boomed, "that is enough!"

And Delly heard it in his voice: Now she was just trouble to Lionel Terwilliger, too.

"Please be seated," he said sternly.

Delly shuffled to her seat and slumped into it. The feeling bad was back, full-blast. It pounded her with, "bad, wrong, trouble" all morning long.

When the recess bell rang, Delly didn't hurry. As she slouched past his desk, Lionel Terwilliger called to her, "Ms. Pattison."

She trudged over.

"There is information I shared with the class, before Ms. Boyd arrived, which you need to know," he said, no warmth in his words. "First, Ms. Boyd does not speak."

"What the—?" she mumbled.

His hand went up. "She can hear, but she does not speak. In addition, she must not be touched."

Delly dropped her head. Now he thought she was so bad, she'd hit a no-talking girl. "I wouldn't fight her," she muttered.

"I was not suggesting you would strike Ms.

Boyd," he replied. "She must not be touched by anyone. Is that understood?"

Delly nodded.

"You may go." He dismissed her.

But she had to tell Lionel Terwilliger, who hadn't given up on her till today, "I didn't mean to—"

"Delaware," he stopped her. Then he said, softly, "I know."

Delly looked up.

"Despite your intentions, however, you injure others. You must learn to..."

Delly watched his mouth, waiting for the words. How could she stop the trouble? How could she be good?

Instead, he sighed. He couldn't help her.

She slunk outside to recess.

Chapter 15

Danny Novello was good-looking. He was good at school, good at sports, and there was good in him somewhere.

But his mouth was mean. He'd ask Delilah Dingham, who was smart in science, "Do you have a mom and dad, or did they make you in a test tube?" He told the Dettbarn twins, who had problems with personal hygiene, "I heard skunks won't get near you." He oinked at Melbert Fouts, who was fat, and Melbert cried.

Everybody was afraid of Danny Novello's mouth. Everybody except Delly.

Danny Novello loved Delly. He loved her

tinyness, and her trouble. He'd loved her since first grade, but his mouth was too mean to tell her.

The love had only festered with time. Soon, whenever he got near her, his heart beat so hard it hurt. Tell her, it pounded, or I'll burst. So, just before Christmas, he decided to declare it. "Best gift she'll ever get," he boasted.

He was so sure of himself, he brought a crowd. "Watch this," he told them, and parked himself in front of her.

"What do you want?" she rasped.

As soon as Delly closed her mouth he smacked it, with a big, fat kiss. He stood there, waiting for her to say, "I love you, too, bawlgrammit."

Delly's eyes went wild. She coughed, like a cat hacking up a hairball. Then she puckered up, too.

Novello closed his eyes for the kiss he knew was coming.

Instead, Delly turned her head and spit the biggest goober those children had ever seen.

The crowd gasped.

Novello's eyes flipped open. "What the. . . ?" he wondered.

And Delly slugged him.

She dropped him, hard. As he hit the ground, air blew out of him, like a popped tire.

She bent down. With her mouth as close to his as it would ever get, she growled, "You try that again, I'll knock you into next week," and walked away.

Tater was still staring at the spot where the spit hit. "Wow," was all he could say.

The crowd giggled.

"Something funny?" Novello hissed.

They all shook their heads.

Danny Novello couldn't stop loving Delly. But he couldn't forgive her for refusing him, either. From then on, most of his mouth meanness went to her.

He was waiting for Delly with a pack of kids when she came out for recess. He and Tater stood in front of her, so she had to stop.

"Hey Danny,"Tater shouted, "it's Ms. Pattison."

"That's no Ms.," Novello yelled, "that's a monkey."

The crowd exploded with laughter.

Delly exploded, with punches. But she was wild; mostly she was pummeling air.

And Novello was laughing. "I feel a flea. A bug's biting me."

Till she got him. In the gut.

"Oof," he exclaimed.

She jumped him and he toppled, like a tree taken down by a tiny lumberjack.

"Ayeeeeee!" he screamed.

He landed with her on his chest. "Open wide," she hollered, "here comes lunch," She cocked her right fist behind her head, all ready to send a knuckle sandwich to his mouth.

Ms. Niederbaum stopped the delivery. She grabbed Delly's arm, then hoisted her off him.

"What the glub?" Delly exclaimed.

"We're taking a trip," Ms. Niederbaum said, as she carried her across the playground.

"How many weeks on Alaska this time?" Delly grumbled.

But they did not travel to Alaska. They went straight to the place big trouble ends up: The principal's office.

As Ms. Niederbaum set her down outside Ms. McDougal's door, she said, "I think you've done it this time."

And Delly, who'd lost her surpresent, her Dellypresent, and Lionel Terwilliger, muttered, "Nothing left to lose."

She was wrong about that, too.

Chapter 16

All afternoon, Delly sat in the chair. "Forgot about me," she snickered.

Then, from down the hall, she heard Clarice's voice. "We're here to see Ms. McDougal."

"It's about Delly," Boomer added.

"Chizzle," Delly murmured. She watched them walk toward her

Boomer shook his head when he spotted her.

"Delly," Clarice sighed, as if the word meant something sad.

Ms. McDougal was at her door. "Mr. and Mrs. Pattison, come in," she told them, and they disappeared.

It was a long time later when the principal called, "Delaware, please join us."

She trudged to the door.

Boomer and Clarice were sitting against the wall. Boomer's eyes were red and his jaw was tight. Clarice was clenching her chair so her knuckles were white.

Delly slumped to her seat.

"I've told your parents about your trip to the river, and the fight at recess," Ms. McDougal began.

"Hunh," Delly mumbled.

"For the rest of the week, you'll have detention, and recess on Alaska. Your parents have decided on a punishment for home."

Boomer's mouth barely moved. "Your room, for a week."

Delly's head popped up. For Dellypunishments, it was puny. "That's it?" she muttered.

It wasn't.

"Delaware," Ms. McDougal continued, "the trouble is chronic. We're not sure this school can help you, and keep the other children safe, too. We think another placement might be better for everyone."

Delly was wondering if that meant Alaska, all day every day, when the principal told her, "We've agreed to give you one more chance to succeed here."

"Huh?" Delly didn't understand.

Boomer explained. "If you mess up one more time, it's over. You go to a new school, for troubled kids."

Delly thought about that. Then she asked, "If I went to this other place, would I stop being bad?"

Ms. McDougal shrugged. "We hope it doesn't come to that."

Nobody'd been watching Clarice, because Clarice wasn't talking. But sounds were coming out of her now. Delly glanced at her mother.

Tears were pouring down Clarice's cheeks, like tiny waterfalls. She was holding in sobs, so they sounded like hiccups.

Delly's heart stopped. This was worse than any trouble. It was the world falling apart. Because Clarice Pattison didn't cry, ever.

Till today.

"Ma," Delly called, trying to stop it.

Clarice turned to her. She didn't speak, but her eyes were asking.

Delly knew what she wanted: She wanted hope. She wanted her to say, "I'll be different, I promise."

But Delly didn't know how to be not-Delly. "Sorry," she whispered.

Clarice closed her eyes. Her head dropped to her chest. She'd given up on Delly, too.

Ms. McDougal stood. Boomer and Clarice walked out of the office with Delly behind them.

They rode in the van without words. When they got home, nobody had to tell Delly to go to her room.

Chapter 17

Delly lay on her bed. In her head, she made a list of the people who'd given up on her.

It was a long one. There was Officer Tibbetts, Clayton Fitch, Norma, and all the friends she didn't have anymore. Just today, she'd added Lionel Terwilliger, Ms. McDougal, and Boomer. And Clarice. Making Clarice cry was the worst of it.

Then Delly added one more name to the list: "Me."

"It'd be better if I wasn't around," she said out loud, so whatever brought surpresents could take her away.

There were two rivers of tears backing up behind

her eyeballs, but she wouldn't let them out. She squeezed her eyes tight, till they stopped stinging.

It was late when RB showed up. He lay down beside her. "Delly," he asked, "are you going to a different school?"

She shrugged, and the bed shook a little.

"Don't go." His voice was cracking like he'd cry.

She shrugged again.

Then RB was shouting, "Just quit getting in trouble. Just quit it!"

"I'm not trying to get in trouble!" she shouted back.

RB knew that was true. "What are you trying to do?" he asked.

She thought about it. "Have fun. Do something good. Except when I fight."

He said it quietly, so she wouldn't slug him too hard, "Maybe you should try something different."

She didn't smack him. Instead, she rasped, "I don't know how to be…not me."

They both lay there for a while.

"Del?" he said.

"Huh."

"You know when I knock on your door and you say, 'Go away, I'm doing something.' And I want to say, 'You're not doing anything. Let me in!' But I don't, I just sit there and wait."

Delly didn't know that.

"Or you know when Galveston says, 'RB, I'm in charge. Clean up this room,' and I want to take Ma's spatula and whap her. But I don't, I just walk away."

Delly didn't know that, either.

"Know what I'm doing instead of whapping?"

"What?" She turned to him, waiting for the words. Finally, somebody was going to tell her how to stop the trouble.

"I'm counting." RB smiled, so proud of himself.

"What?" she screeched.

"I'm counting. You know: One, two, three...It makes me calm down.

"That's what you gotta do, Del. You gotta count," he told her, like he'd solved everything.

"RB." She was talking through her teeth. "I'm in

trouble up to my eyeballs, and you think I should count?"

"Yep," he said, surely.

"RB, bed," Boomer called.

He slid off from beside her. "Will you try?" he asked.

She shrugged.

"Del, please?" And the tears were two seconds away.

"Okay," she agreed, just so somebody else wouldn't be sobbing because of her.

He put his face close to hers. "I know you can do it," he whispered.

"RB?"

"Yep."

"One, two, three..." she counted, like Clarice did when somebody had till ten before trouble.

And he was gone.

"Counting." Delly spit the word. "I'd rather eat worm sandwiches."

In the dark, she tried to think of something else

she could do to be Dellyifferent.

"They could tie me up," she said. "Then I couldn't fight." But she couldn't eat or do her homework, either.

"They could keep me in my room forever," she suggested. Clarice wouldn't leave her alone in the house, though, since she parachuted off the porch roof.

"Forget it. There's no fixing me." She gave up again.

Till she remembered Clarice crying. "Chizzle," she murmured.

Because Delly could take people calling her names, or being sent to a special school. Everybody in the world could give up on her. Except Clarice.

"RB only counts when he gets worked up. That's hardly ever. I'll have to do it every bawlgram second," she complained.

But there was Clarice, her eyes still asking.

"All right, I'll count," she told the darkness. And that's how she went to sleep: "One bawlgrammit, two bawlgrammit..."

Chapter 18

That's how she woke up, too.

She brushed her teeth counting, trudged downstairs counting, crunched her cereal counting.

She counted as Galveston hissed at her, "I heard about you. You'd better shape up."

"567, 568, 569..." her mouth mumbled, while her fingers curled into fists.

"Galveston," Clarice called, "get over here," and pulled her from the table. So the numbers were not truly tested.

She counted to herself on the way to school.

"What are you doing?" RB asked her.

She didn't stop.

"You're counting," he cheered. Then he sang it, "You're counting, you're counting."

"Is it working?" he wondered.

She shrugged.

"It's working! You can stay. You can stay." He ran around her, singing that.

And Delly didn't tell him, "Don't count on it," because it was good to see somebody happy, even if it wasn't her.

Lionel Terwilliger had to ask her every question twice: Once for her to quit counting, and again for her to hear it.

Then, for one sweet moment, there were no numbers. But as soon as she answered, "A spider is an arthropod, not an anthropologist," she'd start again.

It was the most boring morning ever, and when Delly imagined a lifetime of counting, it was like living death. "I can't," she rasped.

Till she remembered Clarice. "4,732, 4,733...," she kept on.

At recess, she took herself to Alaska. "What the glub am I going to look at?" she asked the State of Seclusion.

Because Delly'd done some thinking. There were two ways, she decided, she kept ending up in Trouble Town. One was thinking something would be fun and doing it; the other was fighting. She wasn't sure the counting could keep her away from either of them.

So she scanned the playground, searching for something that wouldn't tempt her with fun or the fight. There was Danny Novello on the basketball court. "Just make me mad," she muttered. Gwennie and Tater were racing. "Too glad." Everywhere kids were playing and shouting. "Too bawlgram fun," she rasped.

Then she saw it: Sitting under a tree, bent over a book, was that Ferris Boyd.

It wasn't fun. And it didn't make her want to fight much. "One," she began.

From 1 to 1,129, she watched the girl turn the page twice. "Like watching ice melt," she mumbled.

At 1,130, some birds flitted by Ferris Boyd. Squirrels ran circles around her.

Delly yawned.

At 1,492, a bird landed on Ferris Boyd's head. It put its beak in her hair.

Delly sat up.

The bird flapped down to Ferris Boyd's shoulder, and hopped along her arm like it was a branch. It perched on her hand.

"Huh?" Delly quit counting.

Ferris Boyd looked up from her book. Then the girl and the bird stared at each other, as if they were having a conversation. Without making a sound.

When they were finished, the bird flew off. The girl went back to reading.

"What's going on over there?" Delly rasped.

The bell rang and Ferris Boyd stood.

The creatures disappeared into the air and across the grass.

"Chizzle," Delly heard herself sigh, like she was sorry it was over. Like it was fun.

"That wasn't fun," she scolded herself. "It was like watching paint dry." And she followed everybody into school.

Sitting at her desk, though, she kept thinking about Ferris Boyd and that bird telling each other things without talking. "1,556, hmm, 1,557," she murmured.

The day went downhill from there.

During Social Studies, the digits dulled her to sleep. Lionel Terwilliger had to shake her.

"One, two, three!" she woke up shouting.

Till she heard the laughs all around her. "Bawlgram counting," she muttered.

But when Novello passed her desk and hissed, "Hey, Smelly," she snarled, "848, 849…," instead of slugging him.

"Mr. Novello," Lionel Terwilliger boomed, "you will write, 'Ms. Pattison's name is Delaware,' one hundred times."

So the numbers were good for something.

She was counting when RB came to her room before dinner.

"Hey," he said.

She nodded.

"You get in trouble today?" he whispered.

She shook her head.

He started singing, "No trouble to-day."

Between 12,345 and 12,346 she told him, "It's like eating cardboard, RB. It's killing me."

"You can do it," he assured her.

Chapter 19

But Delly was drowning in the dullness.

Every day was nothing but numbers; the same ones over and over again. She stopped feeling sunshine. The world turned dingy gray.

Except at recess.

The creatures came as soon as Ferris Boyd sat down. Red and blue and yellow birds danced in the air above her; squirrels played tag beside her.

Sometimes, Delly'd catch herself giggling, "Ferris Boyd, those squirrels ran over your legs," as if she and the girl were friends, as if it was fun. Then she'd remind herself, "This is not fun. It's like watching grass grow."

It was better than counting, though. And for a half hour, Ferris Boyd wasn't the head-down-hunched-over kid she was everywhere else.

Because in school, Ferris Boyd was a disaster. All day long she drooped over her desk, as if her sadness weighed so much she couldn't sit up straight.

"Ms. Boyd," Lionel Terwilliger would say, "please approach the blackboard and complete the problem."

So she'd shuffle to the front of the room, and slouch by the board.

"You may commence," he'd prod her.

She never did.

Finally, Lionel Terwilliger would give up. "Thank you, Ms. Boyd. You may resume your seat."

And she'd slump back to her chair.

Without the animals, Ferris Boyd was a barely-living lump. Like Delly felt all the time now.

After school, Delly counted as she washed desks for detention. The numbers walked home with her. They sat in the back of her head, waiting, while she did her homework. "Counting is the worst Dellypunishment ever." She sighed.

Except for this: Clarice hadn't cried again.

Chapter 20

All week, Brud Kinney counted the seconds till Sunday. At St. Stanislaus, he had a prayer: Please let me see that boy play again, and I won't wreck it.

Sunday morning, he pedaled slowly down the River Road. About a block from the old Hennepin place he heard it: ping, ping, ping, clang. He put his hand over his mouth to keep from shouting, "A-a-all right!"

At the end of the drive, he peeked around the brush. There was the boy, dribbling and jumping and shooting just like before.

Brud laid his bike in the ditch. He snuck behind bushes till he was halfway down the drive. Don't mess me up again, his head warned the rest of him.

Because Brud had a plan: He would watch, still and silent, for a little while. I'll learn, then I'll leave, he decided.

And at first, his body obeyed. While the boy dribbled between his legs and behind his back, Brud's hands stayed still. When the boy ran down the drive, Brud's feet didn't stir.

Then the boy took the ball in both hands and jumped. As he floated through the air, he turned so the hoop was behind him. Blind to the basket, he threw the ball up over his head.

Brud stopped breathing. It was an impossible shot.

The ball didn't know impossible. It soared to the rim, and slid through it.

And Brud Kinney's plan didn't have a prayer. "Oh m-m-man!" he whooped. His arms were pumping the air with happiness.

The boy swung around. His scared eyes spotted Brud, then he was running.

Just like before, Brud needed too much, too fast

from his mouth. "Hey," he hollered, "you p-play real g-g-g-g-"

The boy was at the stoop

Brud tried again. "You play g-g-g-"

The boy reached for the door. It was over.

Brud hit his mouth with his fist to hurt it. "Unh," it cried. He hung his head, and waited for the door to slam on him and his too-basketball-loving body.

It wasn't the words that stopped Ferris Boyd. It was the "g-g-g-": The sound of a mouth that wouldn't speak. It turned her around.

She saw Brud hit himself. She flinched, like she felt it.

When the door didn't bang, Brud wondered if he'd been g-g-ing so loud he'd missed it. He looked up.

There was the boy, on the stoop staring at him.

Brud took a breath. He pointed to his mouth. "H-hard," he said.

And the boy didn't leave, or laugh.

So Brud kept on. "Y-You play real g-g-g-g-"

The "g" got him again. His head went down for good.

Brud didn't see Ferris Boyd walk toward him. He didn't see the pad and pen she took from her pocket till they were under his eyes.

His face went red. I'm so bad at talking, he thought, that boy thinks I have to write. His hands stayed at his sides.

The pen and paper disappeared, then came back. WRITE HERE, was on the page, in pale, skinny letters. They weren't telling; they were asking.

So Brud did. You play real good. I play, too. I was just watching, he wrote.

The boy read it, and glanced at the ground.

Time to go, Brud's head said.

His hand wouldn't listen. Want to play a game? it wrote.

The boy's eyes got scared again. He looked at the house, then Brud. He was weighing which it would be, and Brud could tell the house was winning.

Give it up, Brud's head insisted.

Instead, his mouth said, "I'm B-B-Brud."

The boy gazed into Brud's eyes, like he was reading them, too.

Brud let him.

After a long time, the boy took the pad. H-O-R-S-E, he wrote.

"Your name?" Brud asked

The boy shook his head.

"Oh, the g-g-game!"

The boy nodded. NO TOUCH, he added, in big, dark letters. He held the paper in front of him, like a shield.

"No t-touch," Brud promised.

The boy passed him the ball to begin.

Brud was so happy, he couldn't keep his mouth from yelling, "Yes!"

Before he took a shot, though, he raised his arm, like he was in school.

The boy looked at him.

"Wh-wh-what's your n-name?" he asked.

Slowly, the boy printed, FERRIS BOYD.

Brud's right hand waved, Hi. He smiled, so the tips of his teeth glowed.

Then they played.

It was over before Brud blinked. He got hammered.

It wasn't that Brud didn't make any baskets; he did. It was because, sometimes, he missed. The boy didn't.

Still, even getting skunked, it was the best time Brud'd ever had. Because he got to watch the boy up close, without barreling through bushes.

Brud's last shot bounced off the rim and came back to the pavement. He turned to the boy. "Ag-g-g-gain?" he asked, because he didn't want it to end.

But the boy had vanished. Nothing moved around that place except birds, and a black cat.

So Brud set the ball on the stoop, and headed down the drive. Before he left, though, he turned to the house and raised his hand, See you next week. He wasn't telling; he was hoping.

In bed that night, Brud was having one of his visions. In his head, he and the boy were playing

H-O-R-S-E again, and this time Brud was winning.

"Time out!" he called, and walked over to the boy.

"Hey, I was thinking," he said, "maybe you don't like talking, either. That's why you have that pad. Maybe we don't have to talk, ever."

In his vision, the boy nodded.

And Brud smiled so his teeth glimmered.

Chapter 21

For Delly, Monday meant no more Alaska, no more detention, no more being stuck in her room.

She wasn't Dellybrating, though. "Now I got all kinds of time for trouble," she fretted.

So at recess, she went to Alaska anyway, because it kept her from fun and fighting.

After school, she walked home with RB.

"Want to skip rocks at the river?" he wondered.

"Nope."

"Want to make a worm pie?"

"Un-unh." It was all too fun.

"Want to watch TV?" he asked at the house.

"No," she sighed, because Galveston'd be there,

too, with a fight all ready for her. She trudged to her room, to keep the peace.

And it worked. Till Gal found her. "You're ungrounded, not on vacation," she snarled. "Get downstairs and help us clean."

So Delly did. She got the dustcloth and swished it across tabletops while she counted.

"That's not dusting," Galveston declared. "That's pushing dirt around."

Delly kept swishing.

Gal got in her face. "Get the spray and start over." As she spoke, Galveston did some spraying—of spit, on Delly.

The spit spattered the numbers aside, so there was nothing between the sisters. Except Delly's fists.

"Gal," she growled.

"What?"

Just before she hurled her hand into Galveston's gut, Delly gasped, "I got to go." She ran to her room, and slammed the door between her and the fight she was hankering for.

Gal followed her.

RB was trailing the two of them, shouting, "Delly, count!"

"One, two," she howled.

But Gal was banging, screaming the numbers to nowhere, "You're not done. Get back there and finish!"

Delly had her hand on the knob. In a moment, it would be holding a hunk of Galveston's hair.

And Clarice came home early. "Hey," she called, "where is everybody?"

"Ma," RB answered, "we're upstairs."

"What's going on?"

"Nothing," all three replied.

"Gal, get down here," Clarice summoned her.

Delly heard her sister retreat.

The battle might be over, but Delly knew the war would go on. She'd need a different plan for Tuesday, or Gal would be bald, and she'd be banished to Trouble Town forever.

She fell on her bed, worn out from fighting the fight, and wasted from a week of counting.

After supper, Clarice came to Delly's room. She sat on the edge of the bed.

Delly was so spent, she hardly noticed her.

"One week and no trouble," Clarice said.

"Hunh," she mumbled.

"Delly," Clarice told her, "your dad and I decided that when you have a month of no trouble, you get a Delly Day."

That woke her up a little. "Huh?"

"Whatever you want, for a day."

Delly'd never had Clarice or Boomer to herself, except for meetings with police officers and principals. The part of her that remembered happiness wanted to holler, "Jiminy fipes!" Instead, she murmured, "Hmmm."

"I'm proud of you, Del," Clarice rasped.

Delly'd never heard that before, either. Just like that, those five words filled her up. They inflated her, like a baDellylloon. She wasn't tiny or tired anymore. She was blown up to bursting with Clarice's pride.

Then there were no numbers, only happiness. She was Clarice's again.

"Ma," she said, because the word sounded so good.

Clarice got up. "Good night, Delly."

"Good night," she replied. She fell asleep with her lips curling up to her eyes.

Chapter 22

There was a reason now, a good one, for staying out of trouble. It wasn't the Delly Day, or to keep her mom from crying. It was being Clarice's pride.

Tuesday morning, Delly was still puffed up with it. It woke her with the words, "Ma's proud of me."

But the numbers were backing up behind her happy thoughts. "Bawlgrammit," she muttered, then she let them through. Clarice's pride depended on it.

The numbers were blown up, too. They were fat and fluorescent-colored. They sashayed around her brain singing, "1, 2, 3…"

"Good morning, Ma," she rasped as she came into the kitchen.

"Good morning, Delly." Clarice smiled.

"Who do you think you are—strutting like you're six feet tall?" Galveston hissed.

The numbers trumpeted an attack. "123, 124..." they blared.

Delly high-stepped it to the toaster, and the rest of breakfast went without a hitch.

It was a long day of counting, though, even with Clarice's pride. By recess, Delly and the digits were tiny and gray again.

On Alaska, as birds flapped around Ferris Boyd, Delly thought about after school. It'd be her and Galveston, with only the dinky numbers between them. There'd be hand-to-hair combat; Clarice's pride would be crushed.

"What'll I do?" she mumbled. Everywhere else was fun or fights.

Then the idea slapped her, like a smack to the brain. "Shikes," she exclaimed.

"It'll be just like sitting on Alaska," Delly told herself. "No fun, no fights. And no Galveston.

"Ferris Boyd," she whispered, "I'm following you home."

At the end of the day, Delly watched Ferris Boyd slump out the back door of the school, then she ran to the front. "Go with Cletis," she hollered at RB, "I'll be home later."

RB went pale with worry. "You in trouble?"

"Nah," she said. "I got a project."

"What kind of project?"

Delly told the truth, sort of. "It's about birds and squirrels and stuff. I got to go."

But RB knew her: Those copper curls weren't bouncing because she had a project. They were bound for a Dellyventure.

"Hey," he called, but she was gone.

"What's Delly doing?" Cletis asked.

"Don't know," RB replied. He was going to find out, though.

Chapter 23

Delly sprinted out the back door of the school and across the playground. "No talking, no touching, no fun," she told herself. "Just like Alaska."

She caught sight of Ferris Boyd at the bridge. "There you are," she whispered, and crept along the concrete.

Ferris Boyd clumped out the River Road, while Delly dashed from tree to tree. At the old Hennepin place, Ferris Boyd trudged down an empty driveway and disappeared in the house.

"Chizzle," Delly griped, because all that tailgating had come to nothing.

The door swung open again. Ferris Boyd was on the stoop, with a bowl in one hand, and a basketball in the other.

"Shikes," Delly squeaked, and dove in the ditch. She peeked over the edge.

Ferris Boyd turned to the bushes beside the yard. Her mouth didn't make a sound.

Suddenly, a black cat sprang out of the brush, like she'd called it. It ran across the grass to her.

She sat on the stoop while the cat ate. After, it circled her while she scratched it.

And the birds were everywhere. Just like at school, they swooped around her, but they didn't come too close. "Because of that bawlgram cat," Delly muttered.

The cat stretched out on the stoop. Ferris Boyd walked to the drive with the ball. She bounced it, ping, ping, ping.

"I hate that game," Delly murmured.

Ferris Boyd turned to the basket. She sent the ball to the hoop, like it was easy.

"Whoa," Delly rasped. Because even though she was too tiny for basketball, it was something to see a kid play like that.

The ditch was better than Alaska, because it

wasn't school. But it was hard squatting, squished against dirt. Pretty soon, every bit of Delly was screaming for a stretch.

So she did. A couple hunks of dirt dropped; noises nobody'd notice.

Unless nobody was a bawlgram cat. It raised its head and stared straight at her.

"What are you looking at?" Delly mumbled.

"Rowwwwwr," the cat replied, telling her and Ferris Boyd, too.

The girl quit playing. She followed the cat's gaze to the ditch.

Delly ducked.

Then there was silence. The silence of somebody sneaking up on me in a ditch, Delly thought.

"Shikes, shikes, shikes," she hissed as she crawled in the dirt toward River Bluffs.

Before she got too far, though, she heard that ping, ping, ping again. She stopped, and snuck a look.

Ferris Boyd was back playing ball. The cat was sunning itself.

Then Delly didn't stir.

It was a long time till Ferris Boyd set the ball on the stoop.

"Finally," Delly breathed.

The girl picked up her backpack, and headed to the woods. The cat trotted behind her.

Suddenly, it was quiet. The birds and other creatures had disappeared, like she'd taken them with her.

Delly still had a while till Clarice got home. "I can go face Galveston," she murmured, "or follow Ferris Boyd." It didn't take two seconds to decide.

She crept out of the ditch, and across the grass. She went into the woods.

It was dark in there. She could hear animals up ahead and over her. But there was no Ferris Boyd. No bawlgram cat, either. "What the glub?" she whispered.

There was a path between trees. Delly snuck along it. Alone in the shadows, she got nervous. "Maybe those two are watching me," she muttered. "Maybe they're witches, living in the woods. Maybe they'll fly at me, and turn me into a —"

"Mowrrrr," it howled from above.

Delly shot, like a sunlight-seeking missile, out of the woods. She dove in the ditch. Her head popped up, fists in front of her. "Come 'Mowr' at me now," she dared it.

But there was no furry witch flying at her.

The River Bluffs whistle blew five o'clock. Clarice would be heading home.

"Bawlgrammit, I got to go," she grumbled, and climbed out of the ditch.

As she ran down the road, the corners of Delly's mouth curled. "Ferris Boyd." She laughed, and shook her head.

Because following her wasn't supposed to be fun, but it had turned into a Dellyventure.

Chapter 24

She got home just before Clarice pulled in the drive.

"Hey Ma," she hollered. "From now on, I'm not coming home right after school."

The color left Clarice's face. "Why's that?" she asked.

"I got a project."

That didn't help Clarice. Delly's projects always got a grade of "T" for Trouble. "What kind of project?"

"It's about wild creatures, and habitats." She used Lionel Terwilliger words. "It's me and a girl doing it."

"Is this for school?" Clarice kept at it.

Delly sort of told the truth. "She's in my class. She's new."

If there hadn't been a week of no trouble, Clarice wouldn't have trusted it. But Delly'd been different. "Hmm," she said.

Clarice had more questions, like Who's watching you? and When's it going to be done? Tallahassee was tugging on her, though, "Can I eat at Fern Teeter's?" and Dallas was yelling, "Ma, there's smoke coming from the stove!"

As Clarice ran to the house, shouting, "Dallas, don't touch anything!" the Delly questions disappeared.

"All right then." Delly grinned.

RB came to her room after dinner.

She was lying on her bed, thinking about that invisible Ferris Boyd.

He stood over her with his arms crossed. "So," he said.

"Hunh," she replied.

"You got a project, for real?"

"Yep," she answered.

"What's it about?"

"I already told you: It's about animals and where they live, how they hide in places you can't see them."

He squinted his eyes. "Who's it with?"

"Ferris Boyd," she said. "You don't know her."

But RB surprised her. "The one who's not your surpresent?"

Delly didn't say anything.

"When are you going to be done?" he asked, because he missed her already.

She shrugged. "You better keep walking with Cletis. Now I got to count. 1, 2, 3..." she called out, louder than any questions he could ask.

So RB left. Outside her door, though, he breathed, "You can't get rid of me, Delly."

Chapter 25

Wednesday, the counting was still killing Delly. Then there was recess.

"Jiminy fipes," she giggled as squirrels played Ring Around the Ferris Boyd. But mostly she thought about after school. "I'm going to find where you disappeared to," she rasped from across the playground.

At three o'clock, she watched Ferris Boyd slump out the door, and followed her.

By the time Delly got to the ditch, Ferris Boyd was facing the bushes.

And there was that black cat, sprinting to her.

Bawlgram cat, Delly only thought it.

Still, the cat stopped and turned.

Delly ducked, waiting for it to tattle.

But the only sounds were birds singing, then the ping, ping of a basketball bouncing.

Delly's head popped up. Just like yesterday, that girl was making the ball do things she'd never seen before. "More bawlgram basketball." She sighed.

Ferris Boyd played till Delly's legs were cramping. Finally, she put the ball down, and walked into the woods with the cat.

"Happy Hallelujah," Delly mumbled, and took off. She ran across the grass and into the darkness. "There you are," she murmured.

Up ahead, Ferris Boyd's pale skin glowed, like a ghost. Delly followed the glowing.

The girl and the cat went behind the biggest tree Delly'd ever seen. She waited for them to come out the other side.

They didn't.

Delly snuck up to the tree. She peeked to see if they were hiding behind it. She tippy-toed around it, twice.

Those two had disappeared again.

"Shikes," she whispered.

Lionel Terwilliger had taught about sublimation, how a solid could turn into a gas in an instant. "They sublimated themselves," she breathed.

Delly got nervous. "Maybe they're both ghosts. Or maybe they're super-smelly gas. Maybe they'll suffocate me with their stink and—"

"Rowwwwr," it howled from above. Right where a gas cat would be, before it swooped down and stink-bombed her.

Delly's legs turned faster than a windmill in a tornado. She was all the way to the bridge before she checked to see if something was chasing her.

But there was no gas cat to be seen.

"What the glub?" she rasped. Then she grinned. "Ferris Boyd, you are a mysturiosity."

The whistle blew.

"See you tomorrow," she said to the gas, or ghosts, or whatever Ferris Boyd and that cat had become.

Chapter 26

Back at school, Delly was getting a reputation. A good one.

Tuesday, Lionel Terwilliger stopped at her desk. "Ms. Pattison," he said softly, "your progress is appreciated," and he smiled at her.

On Wednesday, Ms. McDougal came to the classroom. "Delaware Pattison, please stand," she boomed.

"Bawlgrammit," Delly muttered, because nothing good ever came from her being the only kid standing.

Somehow, she'd done something bad. Now they were going to get rid of her in front of everybody. She could hear Novello snickering.

The principal handed her a piece of paper. Delly didn't need to look to know what it was: A one-way ticket to the reDellyformatory.

"Read it, out loud," Ms. McDougal commanded.

It was cruel genius, like making a criminal read the guilty verdict at her trial. But Delly did it.

"Awarded to Delaware Pattison, for Excellent Conduct," she rasped. There was the date and a big gold star. "Huh?"

"Delly," Ms. McDougal announced, "your conduct has been exemplary."

"Smelly?" Novello snorted. "That's a stinking mistake."

Delly was too confused to count. Her hands folded into fists.

Till she heard the principal shout, "Mr. Novello, to my office. Now!"

Delly watched him clump out of the classroom. "That's better than a gold star." She grinned.

By Thursday, Delly's reputation had gotten to gym class.

"We're going to play basketball," Ms. Gerwitz announced. "Now, for captains..."

Everybody raised their hands. "Ooh, ooh," they begged.

Everybody except Delly. And Ferris Boyd.

Because Delly could "Ooh, ooh," till the world ended, and no grownup was going to put her in charge of other kids. Plus she hated that game. She counted instead.

"I already know who I want," Ms. Gerwitz told them. "Put your hands down."

"Gwennie, you have team number one. Tater, team two." Novello got number three. "Our fourth captain is...," and Ms. Gerwitz smiled right at her, "Delly Pattison."

"Bawldoublegrammit," Delly groaned. She knew Ms. Gerwitz meant something good, but making her captain was bad. Now she'd have to play the game, instead of sitting it out. She'd stink up the place with her tiny basketball terribleness.

"Captains, come here and choose your teams,"

Ms. Gerwitz said. "Teams one and two play first, then three and four."

"Chizzle," Delly grimaced. Now she was playing Novello, too.

She scanned the crowd for potential players. They were all watching the other three, pleading, "Pick me, pick me."

There was one kid, though, not looking at anybody. It was Ferris Boyd.

The idea blew up in her brain like a genius bomb. "Holy shikes," Delly squeaked, it was so smart.

The other captains picked first. All the while, kids were yelling, "Ooh, ooh, me, me."

Till it was Delly's turn. The gym went silent.

It didn't matter. In a few minutes, everything would change.

"Ferris Boyd," Delly called out.

There were gasps, then giggles, as Ferris Boyd shuffled toward her.

It didn't matter.

"We're going to be winners," Delly whispered.

With Ferris Boyd on her team, Delly didn't

need anybody else. She was about to tell Ms. Gerwitz, "I'm done," when she got another blast of brilliance.

I'll pick the kids nobody else wants, she decided. Sibyl Salisbury, Chicky Plunkett, Eldon Stank, Melbert Fouts—Delly got every one of them. They slunked up and stood behind her. None of them said, "Thanks."

It didn't matter.

"We'll all be winners," she breathed.

They sat together for the first game. Melbert was gnawing his nails, asking Delly over and over, "What are we going to do?"

"I got it," she assured him.

They huddled before the tip-off. "Here's the plan," she told them. "Ferris Boyd, you stand by our basket. Everybody else, pass it to her."

Ferris Boyd's head jerked up, her eyes popping with panic.

"That's it?" Melbert shrieked. "That's the plan?"

"Bawlgrammit, Melbert," Delly barked, "just get the ball to her. It'll be all right."

"We're dead," Chicky cried. The others nodded.

It didn't matter. In a minute, Ferris Boyd would transform into a swish-shooting machine. Then they'd be shouting, "Hooray for Delly! She made us winners."

Ferris Boyd slumped to her spot.

"Perfexcellent." Delly grinned.

Ms. Gerwitz blew the whistle and the two teams came to center court. "No touching Ferris," she reminded them.

Melbert jumped for the tip-off. He hopped on one foot while his arms flailed around his head.

Novello grabbed it and took it down the court for an easy lay-up. "Your team stinks, just like you," he sneered as he passed Delly.

It didn't matter. Now she had the ball.

Delly Pattison might be too tiny to shoot, but she could dribble. She was so low to the ground other kids couldn't reach her. As she sped down the court she snickered, "You're going down, Nobraino."

"Here, Ferris Boyd. Do your business!" Delly yelled as she threw the ball to her. Then she turned to the hoop and waited for the swish.

She heard shouts. She felt the wind of people whizzing by. She swung around just in time to see Novello put the ball in his basket.

"Delly!" Melbert wailed.

She looked at Ferris Boyd, still slouching. "What the glub happened?" she asked.

"Nothing," Sibyl sighed. "The ball bounced off her."

Eldon was wheezing. "What are we going to do?"

"Do it again," she told them.

"What?" they screamed.

"I said, 'Do it again!'"

Delly got the ball down the court. This time, she stopped a foot away from Ferris Boyd. "Here it is. Take it and shoot," she said, and lobbed it.

The ball hit the girl's hand, then fell to the floor.

Delly picked it up. "Ferris Boyd, shoot!" she hollered, and tossed it at her.

But the girl was a human backboard. The ball thumped off her belly.

And into Novello's hands. He took it to his basket for two more points.

"Time out!" Delly shouted.

The whistle blew.

Delly stood two inches from her. "Ferris Boyd," she whispered, "I'm getting the ball to you. All you got to do is shoot. Just shoot the ball."

Then Ferris Boyd looked at her, with the same sad eyes she'd seen that day in the green Impala. And Delly knew it wasn't going to happen.

The others gathered around, like frightened fawns. "Delly," Chicky gasped, "what do we do?"

Delly didn't know. "Shoot some bawlgram baskets," she told them.

Melbert started sobbing.

"Just try," she said, softly.

So they did.

Ms. Gerwitz cut the game short from mercy. Still, it was a massacre.

"The stink bombs lose," Novello cheered.

"All right," Ms. Gerwitz ordered. "Clean up and get to your class."

Chapter 27

Delly's team left her as soon as the whistle blew. They walked wide around her, like she was a stinking dead skunk in the road.

"Doesn't matter," she muttered; but it did.

She stayed on the court, slumped over. "It was all supposed to change," she mumbled.

The feeling bad that filled her said, "It did. It's worse."

"At least I'm not in trouble," she rasped.

"No, you're not trouble," the bad feeling told her. "You're a loser. And so are those other kids, because of you."

Delly didn't go to the locker room. She didn't

want to see the smirks, or hear the giggles. "I'll just go to class," she decided, "I'll sit there, stinking in my sweat, till three o'clock."

That wouldn't fix it, though. Because tomorrow and every day after, kids would be calling her names, and laughing at her. That's what they did to losers. Counting couldn't keep her out of that many fights.

"What are you going to do about it, loser?" the feeling bad asked her.

Delly didn't know.

Till she heard his footsteps. Her whole body tightened, knowing he was near.

"I can't fight," she told herself, but she couldn't hear it with him howling, "This place stinks, like loser!"

That did it. She grabbed a jump rope off the wall as she stomped toward him. "I'm going to hog-tie you," she snarled, "I'm going to throw you in Clayton Fitch's canoe and send you down the river."

"Try it," Novello taunted her.

She knotted the rope like a lasso, and swung it

over her head. "Hope you like Hickory Corners," she sneered.

And Ms. Gerwitz shut down the rodeo. From her office, she hollered, "Delly Pattison, come over here. Novello, get to class."

Neither of them moved.

"Now," she commanded.

Novello slit his eyes and stamped away.

Delly growled all the way to Ms. Gerwitz's door.

"Delly, look at me," the teacher ordered.

So she did.

"I'm proud of what you did today." Ms. Gerwitz smiled.

"Huh?" Delly grunted.

"Choosing the kids nobody else picks. That was really good. You didn't win, but you did. Know what I mean?"

Delly didn't. "We got killed," she said.

"You lost the game. So what? In my book, you win."

Delly stared at her, to see if she was kidding. "Me?"

"You. You did good."

Being Ms. Gerwitz's good was like being Clarice's pride: Right away, Delly felt better.

"You should get to class," the teacher told her.

Delly turned toward the gym. She wasn't slumping anymore.

"I won," she told the wall as she put the rope back.

"I'm a winner," she said to the ceiling.

She turned to the exit. "I'm goo—,"

And surprise shot her in the air, like a copper-curled basketball. Because there was Ferris Boyd, drooped beside the gym door.

"What the glub?" Delly rasped when she landed.

Ferris Boyd stayed hunched over, like the saddest loser ever.

Delly knew how that felt. Full of Ms. Gerwitz's goodness, she walked over to her. "Hey, Ferris Boyd," she said, "Ms. Gerwitz says we won even if we didn't. Know what I mean?"

The girl didn't glance at her.

Now, as fine as Delly was feeling, that felt bad.

Because she was trying to give Ferris Boyd something good, and the girl wasn't taking it. Again.

So she said, "Ferris Boyd, how come you just keep standing there doing nothing?"

The girl didn't move.

The good feeling was fading fast. And now Delly was remembering how they could have been winners, but for real, if Ferris Boyd had done something besides slouch there.

"Hey," she hollered, "I'm talking to you. How come you didn't take the ball and shoot it? Do you want to be a loser?"

Delly didn't do it to be mean; she did it because she forgot. While she shouted, "Because I know you can do it. I saw you play," she grabbed the girl's arm.

Ferris Boyd's head jerked up, and her eyes were wild. Her arms flailed around her head.

"Shikes." Delly pulled her hand away.

It was too late. Ferris Boyd was running, like wild dogs were after her, down the hall and out the back door.

"Double shikes." Delly followed her. But the girl

was already sprinting across the playground.

"Ferris Boyd!" Delly cried, and headed out the door.

Till Ms. Niederbaum snagged her. "Where are you going?"

"It's Ferris Boyd," she rasped. "She...she's gone!"

"Where?"

Delly pointed.

"Why are you here, and not in your room?"

"I...I was with Ms. Gerwitz," Delly answered, which was sort of the truth.

"Go to your class," Ms. Niederbaum directed.

So she did.

Delly spent the afternoon worrying that they wouldn't find Ferris Boyd, and worrying they would.

"She might be hurt," she fretted. "But if they find her, she'll tell. I'll be out of here before Ms. McDougal can say 'You're expelled.'"

Just before three o'clock, Ms. Niederbaum came to the classroom. She and Lionel Terwilliger whispered.

Delly prepared for her banishment to Badkidville, as Lionel Terwilliger walked toward her.

At her desk, he leaned over. "Ms. Boyd has been located," he said, softly. "She is at her home, and will return tomorrow." Then he put his hand on her shoulder. "Delaware, your awareness and concern are valued." He was thanking her.

Delly wanted to shout, "Happy Hallelujah," because Ferris Boyd was safe and she wasn't in trouble. Yet. But the way Lionel Terwilliger said it, like she was decent, made her hang her head.

"Hunh," she mumbled, and he left her.

Chapter 28

At three o'clock, Delly raced across the playground, over the bridge, and out the River Road. At the end of the drive she checked— there was no car, no cat. And no basketball-playing girl. She ran to the front door of the old Hennepin place and banged on it. "Hey, Ferris Boyd," she hollered, "I got to talk to you."

Nobody came.

"Ferris Boyd, this is a Dellymergency," she shouted.

That didn't do it.

She stood back and looked at the house. The curtains in the upstairs window fell together.

"I got to know if tomorrow's my last day at that school," she muttered to herself.

Breaking in would probably be trouble. Throwing rocks could go wrong, too.

There was one more thing Delly could try. "Tell the truth." She didn't like doing it, but she was stuck. "Bawlgrammit," she grumbled, and sat down facing the house.

"Okay, Ferris Boyd," she told the window, "here's the truth: I'm trouble. I've been bad for a long time." That was hard to say; Delly sat with it for a second.

"I've been better, though," she went on, "so they made me captain. I didn't want to do it. Till I got this idea: You, me, all those kids that got no friends—we could be a team. We could help each other."

The curtains pulled back, just a little. Delly'd have to tell more truths.

"Okay, here's the real truth. I saw you at school with those animals, and it was something. Then I followed you here and watched you play and you were awesome. So when Ms. Gerwitz picked me, I picked you—because I knew, with you on the team, all us losers could be winners for once.

"But then you just stood there. I didn't mean to touch you; I just wanted to know what happened."

The curtain pulled back some more.

"Okay, here's the real, real truth," Delly rasped. "If I do one more bad thing, they'll kick me out of school. I don't care what happens to me," the rasp cracked, "but I can't make my Ma cry again. That's why I need to talk to you."

The curtains closed.

Delly's chin fell to her chest. "Chizzle," she mumbled.

The mail slot in the door creaked open. A small piece of paper slipped through it, and fluttered to Delly's feet.

She picked it up. Big, dark letters told her, NO YELLING. NO TOUCH.

Delly got too excited. "Okay, Ferris Boyd!" she shouted, "I won't—" and stopped herself. "I won't yell," she whispered.

The door opened a crack.

"And I won't touch you," she murmured.

It opened some more.

"Hey, Ferris Boyd." Delly just breathed it.

The girl stepped onto the stoop. She sat down, facing the trees.

Then there was one more truth Delly had to tell. "Ferris Boyd," she said, "I'm sorry."

The girl just stared ahead.

Now, Delly Pattison didn't like apologizing. She had a hard time doing it and getting nothing back. She was about to ask, loudly, "Hey, did you hear me? I said, 'Sorry.'"

And that black cat ran across the yard. It set itself between them. "Mowr," it growled, with all its claws sticking out.

So Delly kept quiet, while the three of them sat.

At first, it was almost as bad as counting, sitting there like that.

But Delly could hear the creatures all around them. She watched Ferris Boyd's back rise and fall with her breaths. She felt the breeze on her face.

The cat stretched out, and put its front feet against her.

Bawlgram cat, she thought, but she didn't move.

Then it wasn't so bad, just sitting. It felt good, not being alone.

The whistle blew. "Shikes," Delly whispered, "I got to go." She stood up.

She sat down again.

"Ferris Boyd," she said, eyeing the cat's claws, "I just got to know—how come you didn't take the ball and shoot?"

The girl stayed still.

This time, Delly didn't push it. "Okay," she said softly.

As she got up to leave, though, Ferris Boyd pulled a pad and pen from her pocket. She wrote something, set the paper on the stoop, and walked in the house.

Delly snatched the note quick, before the cat could claw her.

She sprinted all the way home. Sitting beside her bed, she opened it.

YOU DIDN'T ASK, it told her.

She was silent for a second.

Then her mouth exploded. With laughter. "Ask," she whooped. "Ferris Boyd, I don't ask to do anything."

She held the note in front of her, chuckling at it. "You don't ask to do stuff. You just do it and then… and then…"

She wasn't laughing anymore. "Then there's trouble," she mumbled.

Delly lay down on her bed. She thought about every time she'd gotten in trouble—the chickens, the canoe, the holiDelly days. They were all different, but they ended the same: With her deep in it. "Started the same, too," she rasped. "I didn't ask."

"But I hate asking," she grumbled. "If you ask, they say, 'No.' They never let you do anything."

She put the note in her left pants pocket. It was just paper, but she could feel it pressing on her. "Huh," she said.

"Huh," she kept saying, through dinner and while she did her homework. "Huh."

Sometimes, when Delly couldn't sleep, she'd go to Clarice.

About midnight, she showed up at Clarice's side of the bed. The woman was deep asleep.

Delly crouched so her mouth was near her mother's ear. "Ma," she rasped.

Clarice's eyes flipped open. "Delly," she groaned.

"If I asked Ms. Silcox for brownies, you think she'd give me some?" Delly asked.

Clarice, still groggy, murmured, "Probably so."

"If I asked Clayton Fitch to borrow his canoe, you think he'd let me?"

"No," she told her truly.

"If I asked you if I could take a boat down the river, would you say 'Yes'?"

Suddenly, Clarice was wide awake. "Absolutely not," she shouted.

"What if I asked you to take me?"

That calmed her. "Probably so," she said.

"And I wouldn't have gotten in trouble."

"Nope."

It was quiet. Then Clarice had a question. "Delly?"

"Ma."

"Can I go back to sleep?"

"Probably so," Delly answered.

"'Night, Ma," she whispered at the door.

"Nnnn..." Clarice replied.

Chapter 29

Friday morning, Delly jerked awake. "Bawlgrammit," she gasped, "I didn't ask her not to tell."

"One, please don't tell, two, please don't tell..." she counted as she pulled on her pants. Then she stopped. "She won't tell," she gulped. "She'll write it. Three, please don't write, four, please don't write..." She dashed down the stairs.

She was ricocheting around the kitchen, grabbing her bag and throwing things in her mouth. She had to get to school early and talk to Ferris Boyd, before Ms. McDougal did.

"What's going on in there?" Clarice called.

Any other day, Delly would have hollered, "I'm out of here," and run at the door. And Clarice would have arrested her. "Hold it! You go back to your room and begin again." It would have been ten minutes of starting over, leaving the bad taste of trouble in both their mouths.

But this day, something in Delly's left pocket pinched her. "Ouch," she yelped. She pulled the paper out. You didn't ask, it reminded her.

Delly chewed the mess in her mouth. Then she asked, "Ma, can I go to school early? I got something to take care of."

The question cast a spell on Clarice; she couldn't say "No" to it. "All right," she agreed.

"I'm coming, too," RB announced.

"I'm running," she warned him.

"I know."

They sprinted all the way, burping up their breakfasts. Delly slowed to drop RB at his door, but he didn't stop. So she did.

"What?" she said.

"What what?" he replied.

"Get in there," she ordered.

"I'm coming with you."

The worry was making her wild. She grabbed RB to hurl him into his room. But there it was again, pinching her.

She took a breath. "RB," she asked, "will you let me do this on my own?"

She wasn't yelling or nocussing him. She was being nice. "What's wrong with you?" he wondered.

"Please?" she said.

The questions charmed RB, too. "Okay," he told her.

And she was gone.

Delly stood by the back exit. The first bell rang, but no pale skinny girl showed up. The second bell rang.

"I'll wait," she decided.

Ms. Niederbaum disagreed. "You don't want to be late." She grabbed Delly's shoulder and guided her to class.

"She must be out today," Delly murmured as they got to the room.

But Ferris Boyd was already there, slouched over her desk.

"Shikes," Delly exclaimed, and started toward her.

"Ms. Pattison." Lionel Terwilliger stopped her. "We are ready to commence. Assume your seat.

"Ms. Boyd," he said, "please approach my desk."

Lionel Terwilliger whispered to her, and Ferris Boyd slumped out the door.

She was gone for 1,768 seconds, because Delly counted.

When she came back, she set a note on Lionel Terwilliger's desk.

"Ms. Pattison," he called out, "Ms. McDougal requests your presence."

"Chizzle, chizzle, chizzle," Delly muttered as she trudged down the hall.

They made her sit outside the office through recess, because that was the cruelest thing to do.

When she finally got in, Ms. McDougal took a

deep breath. "Delaware," she said, "you know about Ferris Boyd's disappearance yesterday."

A gurgle came out of Delly, like she was drowning. Her head dropped.

"I've spent time with Ferris this morning, trying to understand what happened," the principal went on. "I asked her why she ran away, but she won't communicate with me about it."

Delly's head popped up.

"As you know, it's unacceptable for a student to leave school. But Delly, Ferris is special, and I've decided to let it go this time. I hope you understand why she's being treated differently than you were."

Delly couldn't believe it—Ms. McDougal was asking if it was okay to let Ferris Boyd off the hook. She nodded and got up to go.

"There's more," the principal told her

She slid down again.

"I'm worried about Ferris, that she's always alone. I asked her if she had a friend she could share with. This was her reply." Ms. McDougal pushed a small piece of paper across her desk.

Delly picked it up. A big, dark NO was written in the middle of it. But there was a line through that. In tiny letters at the bottom the page was, DELLY.

Suddenly, there was a warm spot in the middle of Delly's chest.

"Delly, I am...," Ms. McDougal's voice cracked, like she was choking on it, "proud of you."

Delly choked up, too. "Can I keep it?" she rasped.

"I think that would be all right," Ms. McDougal answered.

Delly put the paper in her right pants pocket. As she walked to her room, the warm spread out to her fingers and down to her toes.

"I got a friend," she whispered to the world, and her mouth couldn't keep from smiling.

Chapter 30

After school, Delly had to run to catch up with her friend. "Ferris Boyd!" she hollered, too happy.

The girl flinched.

"Oops." Delly tried again. "Hey, Ferris Boyd," she breathed, and fell in beside her.

The question paper was pinching her, but Delly wouldn't ask, Mind if I come along? Instead, she said, "Since I don't got too much going on, I guess I'll go with you."

Side-by-side, they walked across the playground, over the bridge, and out the River Road.

When they got to the old Hennepin place, Delly headed down the drive.

Till she noticed no Ferris Boyd beside her. "Hey, where'd you...?" She turned.

The girl was back by the road.

"Ferris Boyd?" Delly called to her.

The girl wouldn't glance at her.

Delly knew what somebody not wanting her around anymore looked like. Her friend was sick of her already. "All right then," she mumbled, and clumped up the drive. As she passed Ferris Boyd, she felt the pinching.

"I won't ask," she muttered.

But the paper pinched so hard, her leg went limp. "Fine, bawlgrammit," she grumbled.

Her throat tightened up so she could hardly speak. "Ferris Boyd," she whispered, "do you want me to go home?"

She couldn't watch for an answer; a nod would hurt too much. She hung her head, and the two of them stood there.

And it was like Delly was one of those birds, and Ferris Boyd was telling her something without a sound. "Oh," she exclaimed.

She gazed at the girl. Then she said softly, "Ferris Boyd, I don't need to come in your house. And I don't want to play ball with you, because I hate that game. I'll just sit on the stoop. How's that?"

The girl stayed still.

Delly let her. It was as if she asked, Will you give me a minute? and Delly told her, Sure, without a word.

Finally, Ferris Boyd tipped her head toward the house. She trudged up the drive.

It was the best "Yes" Delly'd never heard. "All right then." She grinned. She followed her to the steps and sat down.

When Ferris Boyd came out with her ball and the bowl, the black cat leapt onto the stoop. It smelled the air around Delly. "Trrrrrrp," it trilled, and Delly didn't know if that meant, She's okay, or, Let me tear her up.

Ferris Boyd put her hand on the cat's back. It flicked its tail twice, then went to the bowl. When it was done, it lay down beside Delly.

"Bawlgram cat," she breathed, but she didn't pull away.

It was all right, watching Ferris Boyd play basketball. For about a minute.

Maybe Delly did it to pass the time. Or maybe she knew you're not really friends till you know all of somebody, including their trouble.

"Ferris Boyd, want to hear a story?" she asked.

The girl kept playing.

"All right then. Troubletale Number One: The first time Officer Tibbetts tells me I'm BAD."

The cat turned its head to her. The birds quit chattering.

"We went to the Fair," she began. She told about the Poultry Pavilion, and how sad those cooped-up chickens looked. "They were squawking at me, 'Please, please, set us free.' So I did. After, they were prancing around, like they were at a party." She grinned, remembering that.

Suddenly, her face darkened. "Next thing I know, Verena's holding me up, hollering, 'Bad, bad,

bad.' And I was so dumb, I thought she was joking." She glanced over at her friend.

Ferris Boyd wasn't playing; she was watching Delly. Her eyes were blue sadness. But now, the sad was for somebody else.

Delly didn't want it. "It's just a story." She smirked.

Ferris Boyd understood. She started dribbling again.

Delly was quiet for a bit. She'd always hated hearing that story. Somebody'd tell it, and it was all about her trouble, not her trying to help. Telling Ferris Boyd was different, though. Delly didn't feel bad; she felt better.

"Want to hear another one?" she asked

Ferris Boyd took a shot and swished it.

"Troubletale Number Two," she declared, "I'm a brownie burglar."

The whole time Delly talked, the girl played ball. She didn't shake her head or tsk, tsk like everybody else. It was as if, for Ferris Boyd, Delly wasn't horribadible at all.

"You ready? 'Cause here comes Troubletale Number Three." Delly started another one.

And the girl kept playing.

Chapter 31

As long as Ferris Boyd didn't quit, neither did Delly. She got all the way through Troubletale Number Five, and was about to begin Number Six.

Suddenly, the ball stopped bouncing. Ferris Boyd was standing on the steps with her backpack.

"Oh," Delly said. "Hey."

The girl stared off at the woods.

Then Delly realized what she'd done. In less than an hour, she'd told her brand new friend some of the worst things about her. Now Ferris Boyd knew about the tiny ton-of-trouble sitting on her stoop.

But Delly wouldn't ask, "You change your mind

about me?" Instead she said, "I'm pretty bad, huh?" and snickered.

Ferris Boyd didn't look at her. She walked away, to the woods.

And Delly had her answer.

Just like that, the feeling bad was back, beating her up. "You're too much trouble for anybody," it told her. "You can't even keep a friend for a day."

Delly eyes started stinging. She got up to go.

"Rowwwwwwr," the cat yawled at her.

Teeth bared, Delly spun around. "You laughing at me?" she snarled.

Ferris Boyd and the cat were at the edge of the woods. They weren't laughing, though. They were waiting.

"You..." The rasp cracked. "You waiting for me?"

The cat's tail flicked twice, and the feeling bad vanished.

"All right then." Delly sighed and trotted to them. Together they walked into the woods.

In the dark Delly remembered: Soon, Ferris

Boyd and the cat would disappear. Maybe they'll sublimate me, too, she thought, so she stayed close.

They came to the big tree and stopped. Delly got ready for some smoke, maybe a small explosion.

The cat went to the other side of the tree, and was gone.

Ferris Boyd went next, and didn't come back.

"Hey," Delly called, and followed. She walked all the way around the tree.

But there was nothing left of those two; not even a tiny puff of smoke.

"What the glub?" she muttered.

"Mowr," the cat laughed.

"Where are you?" she shouted

"MAOH," it yowled.

Delly looked up. They were staring down at her through the leaves. They weren't ghosts or gas.

"How'd you get up there?"

A pale, skinny hand pointed to the trunk.

Finally, Delly saw it: Chunks of wood were nailed to the side of the tree. They looked like big hunks of bark. "It's a bawlgram ladder," she exclaimed.

She started up it. Step by step, she entered the green, till it surrounded her. Birds called from close by; squirrels ran along limbs as if they were roads.

Way up, boards were nailed to the branches so they made a floor. Delly pulled herself onto it.

And she was in a room, with leaf walls and a leaf ceiling. A railing ran around the outside of it. Ferris Boyd crouched in a corner, with a book against her chest. The cat sat beside her.

The other world was gone. The tree held them, like a giant green cocoon.

"Oh, Ferris Boyd," Delly whispered, "you got a hideawaysis."

The girl's eyes were wondering.

"It's your special secret place," she explained.

Ferris Boyd nodded. She knew.

The sun shone through the leaves, making them glow like jewels. The breeze shook them, so they danced.

Delly stood and turned slowly. There was plenty of room to spread out. "You could eat here," she announced.

There was shade, and shelter. "You could sleep here," she said.

She saw all that space far from everything bad and hard. "You could live here," she breathed.

She kept turning and talking. "You'd never be in trouble, because it's your place. Nobody could make fun of you, because you're in charge."

She had to stop. Something about the hideaway-sis made her heart ache, like she'd been missing it forever. "Chizzle," she sighed, and sat down.

Then Delly was quiet, because there weren't words for what she was feeling. She'd just got a whole new world, because Ferris Boyd had shared it.

At five o'clock, she heard the whistle from the other world. "I got to go," she said, sadly.

"Ouch, ouch, ouch!" she yelped, as she climbed down the ladder. The question paper wouldn't let her leave.

She climbed back again. "Ferris Boyd..." She started, but she couldn't finish. It was the hardest question yet, because she wanted it more than anything.

The paper pinched it out of her, though. "Can I please come back?"

Ferris Boyd glanced at the cat.

The cat stared at Delly.

It's over, Delly figured, if the bawlgram cat decides. She waited for one thump, "No!" from its tail.

Instead, the cat flicked it twice, "Okay," and closed its eyes.

"All right then," Delly rasped, holding the happiness in.

She scampered down the tree. She waited till she was at the bridge to shout, "Happy Hallelujah!" She smiled so big her cheeks hurt.

Back at the hideawaysis, the corners of the cat's mouth curved, just a little.

Chapter 32

That night at supper, Delly didn't count; she thought about the hideawaysis.

When Galveston sneered, "What are you doing—planning your next misdemeanor?" she didn't even hear her.

Because Delly had ideas. As soon as she got to her room, she got a list going. She talked out loud, like her friend was with her. "I got to fix those railings, because they're rickety. And you could use a roof over where you sit.

"We need a blanket, and something for food, and a box with a lock for special stuff.

"It's going to be a fortrastle, Ferris Boyd." She

grinned.

Saturday morning, Delly went to work. She was too busy to count, but she asked about everything.

"Ma, can I take that piece of metal behind the garage?" she inquired.

"Okay," Clarice said.

"Can I have some nails?"

"All right."

"Can I borrow the hammer and saw?"

Now, to the rest of the world, those things were tools. But in Delly's hands, they could be Weapons of Gal Destruction. Clarice had a vision of Galveston going down the river in a Delly-built boat. "What's all this for?" she asked.

"For my project," Delly told her.

"I thought it was about nature."

"We're building stuff, for creatures," Delly answered, almost honestly.

"So you're not doing any hammering near Galveston?" Clarice wanted to be clear.

"Ma," she laughed, like Clarice was kidding, and went out the door.

In the afternoon, RB came sniffing around.

Delly was gathering supplies, putting them in a pile in the garage.

"Hey," he said.

"Hunh," she said back.

"What are you doing with that stuff?"

"It's for my project," she told him.

"When are you going to be done?" he asked for the twenty-third time.

She shrugged, and put a can of screws on the pile.

"Don't you have to get a grade?" RB might be young, but he knew the rules.

"It's extra credit," Delly replied.

And that's when RB knew she was sneaking. Because Delly hardly did her regular homework, let alone extra. Her story stunk, like skunk's spray on a hot summer day.

He slit his eyes, trying to scare her into coming clean.

Delly wasn't worried. She had a friend, and a hideawaysis. She had a new start. "See ya," she said.

So RB left. But he would not be left behind.

Chapter 33

When Delly wasn't working on the hideawaysis, she practiced asking questions.

She discovered the Start Big to Get Small Strategy. "Ma, can I have ten bucks?" was the too-big beginning.

"No," Clarice answered.

"Can I have five?"

"No."

Then she got to where she wanted to be. "Ma, can I please have a dollar to go to the store?"

By then, a dollar seemed like a deal to Clarice. "All right," she agreed.

She invented the Wear Them Down with Questions Technique.

"Dallas, can I have some of that candy bar?" She pointed at the one he was unwrapping.

"No," he told her.

Instead of fighting for it, she asked, "Don't you want to give me some?"

He didn't.

"You sure?" she stared at him, big-eyed like a begging dog. "Please?"

That broke him. "Here," he sighed, and gave her half.

"Thanks, Dallas," she said, and they ate side-by-side.

The questions worked with Galveston, too.

Delly'd been sweating all morning, hauling stuff for the hideawaysis. At lunch, when Clarice got up to make more grilled cheese, Galveston hissed, "You smell like pig perfume." She waved her hand in front of her face, like she couldn't stand the stench.

But instead of whomping her, Delly whapped her with a question. "Gal," she whispered, "how'd you like a dead squirrel under your pillow?"

That silenced her.

"Ha." Delly smirked.

By Sunday evening, though, Delly's brain was spent from coming up with all those questions. So when Galveston barked, "Delly, these dishes are still dirty. Do them again," she didn't have anything left to ask her.

She tried counting. "One, two…"

Gal wouldn't quit. "I said do them again. Now," she commanded.

And Delly was a Galveston-seeking missile, ready to blast off and blow. Just before she did, though, she spotted Clarice through the window. *Give me something*, she begged her brain, *before I mess up.*

As Gal came at her, hollering, "Did you hear me? I said…" Delly's brain spit out the only question it had left. "Galveston," she shouted, "do you hate me?"

Galveston's eyes flashed. Her lips curled in an awful grin. "Yes!" she yelled.

The "Yes" hit Delly hard. It knocked the wind out of her.

Because, while Delly didn't like Gal much, she didn't hate her. Delly loved Galveston like liver and onions on Tuesdays—it was always bad, but it was part of being a Pattison. And she loved that a lot.

She took little breaths, because the hate hurt too much.

But Gal wasn't finished. She planted herself in front of her.

Delly flinched, like a dog that had been kicked but couldn't get away.

Gal squinted her eyes. "I..." she growled. "You..." she grumbled. Finally, she muttered, "I don't hate you."

"For real?" Delly rasped.

Gal let out a breath, and Delly could feel the heat of it. "Sometimes I hate what you do," she mumbled.

That hit Delly, but not so hard. Sometimes she hated what Gal did, too.

Galveston kept going. "You're always getting

into trouble. You're always making Ma upset, and getting Dad mad. It's always about you and your trouble, and I hate it." It was the truth behind every mean thing she'd said.

There was a big quiet between them. Then Delly whispered, "Sometimes I hate what I do, too, Gal."

"Then why don't you stop?" she asked.

"I'm really trying," Delly told her.

Galveston thought about that. "I know." She nodded.

"Gal, will you..." Delly started, but she couldn't finish. She couldn't ask her sister to quit tormenting her, to act like she loved her just a little. The "No" would hurt too much.

Gal heard her anyway. "Okay," she said. She looked at Delly, and her eyes had something like love in them, liver and onions love.

"Okay," Delly breathed. Because liver and onions was never going to taste good, but she wouldn't give it up for anything.

Chapter 34

Sunday, Brud Kinney was up with the birds.

He rode down the River Road, listening for the sounds of a boy and a ball. When he heard the ping, ping, ping, his legs pedaled like they were nuclear-powered. He dropped his bike in the ditch and ran to the drive.

The boy heard him. He stopped and held the ball to himself.

Brud had bought a small pad and a pen at the IGA. He took them out of his pocket.

Want to play? he wrote.

The boy got his pen and pad. H-O-R-S-E, he answered, NO TOUCH.

How about M-O-N-K-E-Y? Brud's paper asked.

Now Brud Kinney was no fool. He'd made M-O-N-K-E-Y up, so he could play one letter longer.

The boy looked at Brud. There was something different in his eyes, like a laugh. He walked away, dribbling the ball.

Brud didn't know what that meant.

The boy stopped where the foul line would be. He raised his arms, and sent the ball through the air. It was beautiful. It was a basket.

He stood to the side of the drive. He was waiting for Brud.

Brud was so happy, his legs wanted to jump and his mouth wanted to wh-wh-whoop. Just shoot the ball, his head said.

So he went to the spot. But Brud had too much happiness in him; he was wild with it. His shot went up, up into the sky, like a satellite. It landed on the garage roof, and bounced into the woods.

Brud fetched the ball. Then he ran behind the garage to unleash some of the happiness. He jumped ten times. He "Whooooweee"d into his hands.

That'll do, his head decided.

His feet were still bouncing, though, as he walked back to the drive. He passed the ball to the boy.

Ferris Boyd shot from the same spot and sank it.

Brud tried again. The ball thumped against the backboard and clanged through the hoop.

"Y-yes," he whispered, and his feet did a little dance. This time his head didn't try to stop it.

It was longer till Ferris Boyd finished him off. Not just because it was M-O-N-K-E-Y, but because Brud was better.

Still, that basketball-loving Brud wanted more. As soon as the game was over, he sprinted to the boy. He stuck his pad in front of him. Again? it read.

The boy stopped at the stoop. He looked at the note, then at Brud.

It was a while waiting. Brud didn't mind. He'd wait forever, if it meant more basketball.

Finally, Ferris Boyd turned to the drive.

Brud knew what that meant now. He was too happy again. He bolted behind the garage. "Y-y-yahoo!" he hollered into his hands.

When he came back, his smile was so big the two teeth were beaming. Ferris Boyd had to squint to see him.

Quit that, his head said, but Brud couldn't stop.

After he got M-O-N-K-E-Y, Brud raced to the stoop to try for one more game.

Just like before, though, Ferris Boyd had vanished. There was nothing but birds and that black cat around.

That was all right. Brud'd had all morning playing ball with the boy. He waved once at the door, See you next Sunday.

He rode into town grinning. The two teeth gleamed, almost blinding anybody who looked at him.

Chapter 35

Monday morning, Delly packed two extra sandwiches. She put the hammer and nails in her bag, and she carried a couple of boards.

"Those for your project?" RB asked.

"Yep."

"Hmm," he said.

At school, Ferris Boyd still kept to herself, and Delly didn't push it. She could take being alone and counting at school, if she had her friend and the hideawaysis after.

Plus Delly was busy. She did her work, she wrote lists of supplies they'd need for their place, she drew diagrams of it all fixed up.

She counted when other kids were around, but now the numbers danced to a tune, "I got a friend, and a hideawaysis, too. After school I'm going there, so ya-ah-hoo."

At recess she went to Alaska. She brought paper and a pencil. "I'll design a Dellyvator," she decided.

It had been a while since Delly and Danny Novello had gone at it. Too long for Novello. He missed her torturous touch.

He circled Alaska. "Dinky," he sneered, "I could smell your stink from the steps."

She set the paper down and started counting, "One, two, three..."

But Novello would have her. "I'm going to build you an igloo. I'll call it Smelly's Alaskan Stinkhouse," he shouted

Even with the counting, Delly's fingers curled into fists. She glanced at the Dellyvator drawing. All the plans would be finished with one fight.

She searched the playground for something to save her. Ms. Niederbaum was nowhere. But there was Ferris Boyd.

Delly leaped off Alaska. She raced toward the girl who'd shown her a world without trouble.

And he followed, like a giant gnat buzzing after her.

When they were ten feet away, Ferris Boyd glanced up and saw them hurtling toward her. Her arms flew in front of her. STOP, they said.

So Delly did. She flung herself on the ground beside her. "Help," she begged.

Ferris Boyd's arms dropped, and she stared at Delly. She was telling her something, without words.

Delly couldn't catch it, though, with him screaming, "They got a chair for you in detention. It's called Stinky Dinky's seat."

She threw her hands over her ears, and closed her eyes. She had one second till she pounded him into tomorrow.

Then she heard it, under all the noise. She felt it, pinching in her pocket.

She jumped to her feet and faced him. "Novello," she hollered, "do you want me to hit you?"

He was so surprised by the question, he could only tell the truth. "Yes," he howled. "Hit me!" Then he remembered his meanness. "I'd like to see you try, pipsqueak," he sneered.

But it was too late. Now Delly knew: He wanted her to pummel him.

"No," she told him.

"No?" he shrieked. "You afraid Smelly? Because you know you can't do it. You can't touch me."

Delly wasn't afraid, though. She was free. She walked back to Alaska.

He trailed her, taunting, "Try it. Come on, Smelly."

There was more yelling, then, from Ms. Niederbaum. "Novello, to the steps!" she commanded.

Delly sat on Alaska, smiling. Not because Novello was incarcerated, although that was nice. Because, for once, she was free of the fight.

All afternoon, she Dellybrated at her desk. If the questions could keep her from pounding Novello, maybe she didn't need the numbers at all. She banished them to the back of her head. In their place, she had a song: "I don't need counting; I got questions, instead. And I don't fight. Yep, I'm doing all right."

After school, Delly ran to Ferris Boyd. "Hey," she said softly, and fell in beside her, like they'd been friends forever.

She waited till they were at the bridge to ask, "Ferris Boyd, did you see? I didn't fight." Then she told her, without saying a word, I heard you.

Ferris Boyd stopped, and turned to Delly. Her eyes were still sad, but there was something else in them. Something like a smile.

It was only a second. Her head went down again, and she was shuffling along the road.

It was all Delly needed. Ferris Boyd had heard her, too. "All right then." She smiled.

Chapter 36

At the old Hennepin place, Delly was still telling Troubletales. Every afternoon, she'd take her spot on the stoop while Ferris Boyd got the bowl and the ball, and that bawlgram cat came running.

"Hey, Ferris Boyd," she'd ask, "how about we skip basketball and go straight to the hideawaysis?"

But Ferris Boyd wouldn't hear it. She'd go to the drive and start making magic with that ball.

"Okay," Delly'd say, as if she'd warned her, "Troubletale Twenty-Two: The Nocussictionary," or, "Troubletale Thirty-Six: The St. Eunice's spitting contest."

And her friend would keep playing, as if Delly

could say, "I got three heads, and a horn growing out of my back end," and it wouldn't change anything.

Later on, they'd head to the hideawaysis. Ferris Boyd would settle into her corner with her book and the cat curled beside her.

Delly'd bring out the food she'd brought to fatten up her pale, skinny friend. She set two sandwiches between them. "Ma says I got to eat more, so I'll grow," she told her, which was sort of the truth. She'd eat half of one and groan, "I can't fit another bite. Ferris Boyd, will you eat it? Or I'll get in trouble."

The girl stared at the food, then Delly.

"Please," she'd beg. She pushed it toward her. "Now I got to get to work."

While Delly hammered she'd glance over, and Ferris Boyd would be eating behind her hands. "All right then," she whispered.

That first week, Delly fixed the rails around the hideawaysis. "So no people fall out," she told the cat, and it flicked its tail at her. She nailed the piece of metal on top of two branches, and Ferris Boyd had a roof. "Now you won't get wet," she said. She put the cooler in a corner. She brought a box with a lock, and a blanket. "Oof," she grunted as she hoisted them up the tree.

Friday, when she was finished, Delly walked slowly around the place. She touched the rails, the roof, the bark and the branches. She sat in the corner across from her friend. "What do you think, Ferris Boyd?" she asked softly.

The girl gazed at all Delly had done, and her eyes were not sad; they were smiling.

Delly leaned back against the rail. "All right then," she rasped.

The cat walked over to her. It turned in a circle and lay down with its soft back against her leg, like she belonged.

And Delly Pattison, finally peaceful, fell asleep.

She woke to the cat's tail whapping her. "Huh?" She yawned.

She heard the whistle from the other world. "Chizzle," she sighed, and crawled to the ladder.

"See you Monday, Ferris Boyd," she said. She didn't ask, because now she knew: She belonged there, too. "And I'll see you," she told the cat.

The cat turned away like it didn't care, but its tail flicked twice at her.

Then she was running, through the woods, down the road and into town, smiling so the wind whistled through her teeth.

Chapter 37

Sunday morning, Brud Kinney's pad was already open as he walked down the drive. He held it up to the boy.

G-I-R-A-F-F-E, it read. NO TOUCH.

Ferris Boyd nodded.

Brud's happiness ran him behind the garage. "Y-y-yes!" he hollered into his hands. His fists pumped the air five times before he could begin.

And Ferris Boyd whooped him.

As soon as he got the E, Brud sprinted toward the boy, trying to get another game before he vanished.

But the boy wasn't running away. He was standing in the drive with his pad flipped open. AGAIN, it read.

Brud's teeth flashed bright white.

After he got beat, Brud turned to the house, expecting to see the door slamming for his "Goodbye."

Instead, Ferris Boyd was sitting on the stoop.

So Brud walked over. He pointed at an empty spot.

The boy nodded.

Brud sat down beside him.

Brud was used to sitting with someone and not talking. He wasn't used to the other person not talking, too.

He liked it, a lot.

Because people were always talking at him, like it was nothing, and wanting him to talk back. But it wasn't nothing to Brud. It was hard, and he hated it. He hated sounding wrong, and feeling stupid. That never happened with Ferris Boyd.

They sat like that for a long time.

In the quiet, Brud could hear the birds. He

could see them, too, swooping around the stoop. That's a lot of birds, he thought.

And one flew straight at him.

"H-h-hey" he hollered, and ducked. He glanced over at the boy.

The bird was perched on Ferris Boyd's shoulder, like it lived there. "Whoa," Brud breathed.

Ferris Boyd and the bird were staring at each other. Neither one of them made a sound, but Brud could feel it: Those two were telling each other things.

"Wh-wh-what the...," he whispered.

The bird gazed at Brud and started chirping. It was telling him something, too.

Brud heard it, in his head. My friend, it said.

Brud looked at the boy. Mine, too, he thought.

Ferris Boyd turned to him, as if he'd talked. The blue eyes were surprised, then settled into softness.

Mine, too, Ferris Boyd told him, without saying a word.

The bird flew off.

But those two stayed, sitting in the warmth of the day and all the things they didn't have to say.

Chapter 38

RB Pattison had had enough.

He'd walked home every day with Cletis. He'd watched Delly stash things away, then haul them to school. He'd seen her be happy without him.

He'd given her all kinds of chances to come clean. "When's your project going to be done?" he asked.

"For the 122nd time, RB" she hollered, "I don't know."

But mostly, he missed her. He wanted her back.

Monday morning, before they left the house, RB told Delly, "You go ahead. I'll catch up."Then he smiled with just his lips, no teeth showing, which was wrong.

Delly was too busy thinking about the hideawaysis to notice. She took off.

He caught her at the corner. He didn't speak all the way to school.

At his classroom door, she started to say, "RB, you'd better keep walking with C—"

But he cut her off. "I know. Walk with Cletis. You got your project."

That struck Delly as strange, but not enough to stop her. "See ya," she said.

"Yes you will." He smirked.

At three o'clock, RB ran to Delly's class. He hid beside the garbage can in the hall. He waited till Delly passed him, then silently fell in behind her.

He followed the copper curls as they bounced to the back door. Outside, he saw her sprint toward that pale, skinny girl. He watched them go on together.

He could see Delly's arms waving. He could tell she was having a good time. With somebody else. "You," he whispered to her so far away, "you got a friend." He'd never been so lonely.

Then RB tailed them, across the playground, over the bridge, to the River Road.

Those two were moving so fast, they didn't notice the tiny boy tearing after them.

Delly was telling how Novello had tried to trap her again. "He was dogging me, Ferris Boyd, calling me 'Little Delly with the Big Smelly'. So I asked him, 'Do you want Ms. Niederbaum to send you to the steps?'

"'Ms. Need-a Brain?' he says. 'She'd have to grow one first.'"

"And there's Ms. Niederbaum, right behind him." Delly was laughing so hard, she had to quit walking.

For one second, she was standing in the road.

The next second, she was flying.

RB'd built up so much speed chasing those two, he couldn't stop himself. He plowed into her.

The Pattisons bounced off each other like rubber balls. RB landed on his behind. Delly ate dirt.

"What the glub?" she muttered. She flipped over

to see what had slammed her. "WHAT...THE... GLUB?" she hollered at him.

RB was stunned, but not sorry. "What the glub?" he shouted. "What the glub you!"

They came at each other, yelling so loud their lungs hurt, "You're supposed to be with Cletis!" and, "You said you had a project!"

Still, Delly heard it: A scream without a sound. She turned and there was Ferris Boyd, eyes bugging and ready to bolt.

"Stop," she told RB.

He followed her gaze to the scared girl, and was quiet.

Delly only had a moment. "Ferris Boyd," she said gently, "this is my brother, RB."

The girl's eyes were wild, but she stayed.

"Sometimes we get mad," Delly explained. "It doesn't mean anything."

Oh yes it does, RB wanted to wail. It means you lied, and left me... But he didn't, because of the girl.

"We hardly ever fight," she went on. "I..." Delly

didn't want to say it, but she would for her friend. "I love him."

Delly put her arm around his shoulders, and now RB's eyes were bugging. "We're sorry," she said.

Ferris Boyd looked from one Pattison to the other. They had the same skin, and smallness. There was a softness between them. She relaxed a little.

And with Delly's arm around him, the anger ebbed out of RB.

Till she said, "RB's going home now, so we can get to our project."

"I am not going home!" he roared.

Delly glanced at Ferris Boyd; she was getting skittish again. "Bawlgrammit, RB," she hissed, "what do you want?"

"I just want..." He started, but it was too hard to say. Because under all the angry, he just wanted her.

He turned to Ferris Boyd. "I want to come with you," he whispered. In his eyes was all the sadness of knowing that, even if Delly could be without him, he couldn't be without her. Ferris Boyd saw it.

Delly did, too, but she knew two Pattisons would be too much for her friend. So she said, "RB, you can't. She doesn't like people being close and..."

RB couldn't hear her. He and Ferris Boyd were staring at each other, having one of those silent conversations.

Then he asked, out loud, "Can I come with you?"

Ferris Boyd looked deep into him. She nodded once, and started walking again.

"Huh?" Delly about dropped over.

"She said 'All right,'" RB cheered, and went to follow her.

"Hold it." Delly grabbed him. "You got to know the rules." She wasn't going to let him wreck it.

"Okay." He smiled.

"First, she doesn't talk."

"Hmm," he said, because Ferris Boyd had already told him something.

"And no touching."

RB looked at Delly as if she was teasing.

"You can't touch her. She goes wild."

"Okay," he agreed.

"And what I say goes."

He pursed his lips, like that was too sour to swallow.

"What I say goes," she warned.

"And Ferris Boyd," he added.

"She doesn't talk," she reminded him.

"Yes she does. Just not like you."

Delly couldn't argue with that. "All right then," she said, and they ran to catch up with the girl.

Chapter 39

At the old Hennepin place, Delly sat on the stoop. She pointed to the spot beside her. "Sit here," she told him.

So he did.

Ferris Boyd got the bowl and her ball, and the cat came running. At the steps, it stopped and sniffed the air around RB.

"That's the bawlgram cat," Delly introduced them.

"Mowr," the cat cried.

RB smiled. "Hello, Mowr. I'm RB."

The cat flicked its tail twice, and went to the bowl.

Ferris Boyd was dribbling the ball in the drive.

"She plays basketball?" RB whispered.

"Every day," Delly groaned.

They watched for a while.

"She plays ball like you spit," RB told her.

Delly nodded.

"What do you do while she's playing?" he asked.

"Tell stories."

"What kind of stories?"

"Troubletales."

He just stared at her, so she started. "Troubletale Fifty-Six: I parachute off the porch roof and get grounded for a month."

Maybe it was because RB was there. Or maybe it was because she wasn't just trouble anymore, and it was time to talk about something else. Whatever it was, Delly couldn't go on.

"I'll tell a story," RB offered. "RB Story Number One: Our dog, Tuba. Remember Delly?"

"Yep." She smiled.

"How'd we get Tuba?" he asked her.

"She was running in the road, and Dallas brought her home."

"And he named her Tuba because she sounded like a big, loud horn," RB recalled.

"Oof oof oofoofoof," Delly demonstrated.

RB giggled, then he began. "One day, me and Cletis were at the park. Danny Novello and Tater came over to us. 'Want to try something fun?' they asked, and we said, 'Yep.' So they took some rope, strung it through our belt loops, and threw it over the bar that holds the swings. They pulled on the ropes so we went up in the air.

"At first, me and Cletis were laughing, 'cause it felt like flying. Then they made us go up and down so fast our stomachs got sick. 'Stop!' we shouted.

"But they wouldn't. Cletis was about to throw up, when we heard, 'Oof, oof, oofoofoof.' 'Tuba!' I yelled. And there she was, running at us, with Delly behind her.

"'Let them go!' Delly hollered. 'Make me,' Novello said. So Delly ducked her head, and rammed him in the stomach with it.

"They dropped us then. 'Come on!' she yelled, and we ran to the river. Delly taught us to skip stones. Tuba kept running in the water, trying to catch them. Remember?"

"Yep." Delly did. They were both grinning.

The Pattisons were so busy being happy, they didn't notice Ferris Boyd waiting. She put her pad in front of them. TUBA? it read.

"She was old." RB sighed.

"She went to sleep on Dallas's bed," Delly rasped, "and she didn't wake up."

Now they were all sad. But it didn't feel so bad, being sad together.

Ferris Boyd stared into the woods. She passed her pad to them. ANOTHER, it read.

RB understood. "Tubatale Number Two: Tuba gobbles up Gal's birthday cake."

Delly laughed, just hearing the title.

Ferris Boyd went back to playing. She only stopped to ask for more.

Then RB told, and Delly listened, and she didn't mind. It was good, thinking about Tuba instead of trouble. It was good, being together.

Chapter 40

It was time to go to the woods.

"Where are we going?" RB asked.

"To the hideawaysis," Delly answered.

"Oh," he said, because he didn't want to seem too little to know what a hideawaysis was.

RB was last in line. In the dark of the woods, he got quiet. "Delly," he gulped. He didn't say the "I'm afraid" part.

She heard it anyway. "Come on," she said, and let him pass her. She grabbed the back of his shirt so he'd know she was there.

They got to the giant tree and stopped.

"Now what?" he whispered.

Delly looked at the cat, and it climbed. Ferris Boyd followed it.

"Now you," she told him.

"That's high," he worried.

"I'll be behind you," she promised.

So he started up. Ferris Boyd put her head over the edge, showing him where to go.

"Pull yourself onto the boards," Delly hollered when he reached the top.

By the time she got there, he was standing, turning around and around. "Wow," he breathed.

Ferris Boyd was in her corner, with her book and the cat.

"It's a hideawaysis." He sighed.

"Ferris Boyd's hideawaysis," Delly told him. She emptied her backpack. She put the sandwiches between them.

"You got food, too," he sang.

Delly closed the eye her friend couldn't see. "Ma's trying to get me to grow, but I can't eat it all. Ferris Boyd's helping me out." The eye kept winking. "You and I will split this one."

RB couldn't wink, but he blinked five times while he said, "Okay. I'm full anyway," and patted his belly like Santa Claus.

They sat in a circle eating the sandwiches, with RB humming the whole time.

When they finished, Delly put on her pack.

"Where are you going?" he asked.

"To get rocks."

"How come?"

"So if something tries to get us, we got ammunition," she explained.

She was halfway down the tree before she realized he wasn't with her. She climbed back up.

He was sitting about two feet from Ferris Boyd, taking books out of his bag.

"RB, come on," Delly commanded

"No thanks," he answered, smiling.

Now, RB Pattison never turned down a chance to tag along with Delly. "How about you come with me?" She tried again, with her teeth clenched.

"I'm staying with Ferris Boyd," he replied.

Delly didn't like it, him being so close to her.

She thought about dragging him down the tree, but that might set the girl off. "Don't be a bugbotherer," she warned.

"I know." He waved.

So Delly left. She scourged the woods for stones. She hauled them in her pack, then piled them around the edge of the hideawaysis, like cannonballs.

And she checked on RB.

The first trip back, he'd scooched a little closer to Ferris Boyd. But the girl wasn't fussing, so Delly let it go.

By the next time, though, there wasn't six inches between them. RB was squinting over at Ferris Boyd's book, like he might need to get next to her.

"Hey," Delly snarled.

He looked up.

"No touching," she mouthed at him.

"I know," he mouthed back.

Delly only needed one more load of rocks—extra large ones for extra large invaders. "I'll go fast," she decided, and scrambled down the ladder.

It took longer than she figured. The rocks were so heavy, they were pulling her down as she tried to climb the tree. "Oof," she groaned as she flopped onto the floor. She looked up, and then she saw it.

RB Pattison had left his book, and was reading Ferris Boyd's. He had his head on her shoulder and was leaning against her like he lived there.

"Holy shikes," she breathed.

Ferris Boyd wasn't flipping out, though.

He must've snuck up slow, so she doesn't know he's there yet, Delly thought. She had to get him off, quick.

Delly tried to rise, but the rocks flattened her to the floor. So she slid, like a snake with boulders on its back, across the floor to snag him.

Just then, Ferris Boyd glanced up from her book. She gazed at the boy beside her.

"It's over," Delly gurgled.

But Ferris Boyd's eyes didn't go wild. They rested on RB's face. He looked up at her and smiled. Then they both went back to the book.

And Delly didn't even whisper, "What the glub?" She wouldn't wreck it.

Finally, she got the pack off her back. Quietly, she piled the rocks while they read. Then she sat across from them, watching the peacefulness.

Chapter 41

When the whistle blew, Delly said softly, "RB, we got to go."

He crawled to the edge of the hideawaysis. "That's a long way down," he gasped.

"I'll go first," she told him.

One Pattison, then the other, climbed on the ladder.

Ferris Boyd stayed at the top of it. Delly could feel her telling him things without talking. When they got to the bottom, she was gone.

That's when Delly grabbed RB by the shirt and shook him. "Why were you touching Ferris Boyd?" she barked.

"I wasn't," he replied.

"You were leaning against her."

"I know. Touching is this." He took his finger and poked her with it. "I didn't do that."

"Jiminy fipes," she growled, but she couldn't stay mad. He'd gotten Ferris Boyd to let somebody near her.

"We got to run," she ordered.

So they did.

They were on the bridge when Delly slammed to a stop. "Shikes," she howled. "Nobody knows where you were!" Clarice would be calling the police. "We're dead," she groaned.

RB pulled up beside her. "No we're not. I told Ma I'd be with you." He grinned. "Helping with your project."

"When'd you do that?"

"This morning, after I said, 'Go ahead.'"

Delly was impressed with his sneakiness. But now she needed to tell him he couldn't come again; she couldn't risk it. "Hey, RB—"

And RB interrupted her. "Delly," he declared,

"I love you, too." He shot it, like a giant love bullet, straight into her heart.

It blew her heart up. It blew the words for keeping him away out of her mouth. "Shikes," was all she could say.

Then RB was running again. "Come on," he hollered.

So she did.

As soon as Clarice got home, RB told her, "Ma, I'm working on Delly's project every day now."

"Oh yeah? When's this project going to be done?" She asked Delly, but RB answered.

"Don't know. Might be a lo-o-o-o-ong time."

"That's all right with your teacher?" she wondered.

They both nodded, because Ferris Boyd was teaching them things.

And Clarice Pattison, hearing Montana howl, "Ma, the washer's bubbling over!" let it go at that.

Chapter 42

Tuesday at three o'clock, RB raced to the back of the school. "Hey," he greeted the girls, and held the door for them.

"Jiminy fipes," Delly mumbled, but she liked it.

At the old Hennepin place, RB told Tubatales while Ferris Boyd played ball. Delly and the cat listened, with their mouths curling.

And in the hideawaysis, when Delly brought out three peanut butter sandwiches, RB got something out of his pack, too: A jar of marshmallow fluff. He set it between them.

"Shikes." Delly ogled it. "Where'd you get that?" Because Clarice didn't keep it in the house.

"I bought it, with my birthday money," he answered.

"For us?"

He smiled and nodded, like he'd given her Christmas.

Delly felt a banging in her chest. It was pride, thumping through her.

"What do you want to do with it?" she asked, because it was his.

"Put it on the sandwiches," he decided.

She opened them up, and set the slices in front of him.

He took a spoon from his bag. He dropped a big gob of fluff on each slice. When he put the bread back together, the fluff squeezed out to the crusts.

"Sweet cloud sandwiches." Delly sighed.

RB passed them around.

Delly smacked her lips like she'd kiss hers. Ferris Boyd's eyes were wide with wonder.

"One, two, three," RB called out.

Altogether, they bit into the fluffy deliciousness.

"Mmmm," the Pattisons hummed and gobbled.

But Ferris Boyd took tiny bites. She chewed and chewed like she didn't want the taste to leave her tongue.

"Hey RB," Delly asked when they were done, "what are you going to do with the rest of that?" Because there was half a jar left.

He thought about it, then he grinned. "Put out your hands."

So they did.

He plopped giant gobs of fluff onto their palms. They licked it till it was gone. It left their skin sticky.

Then RB and Ferris Boyd lay down, with their fluff-filled bellies in the air.

Delly went to the ladder.

"Where are you going?" he asked sleepily.

"To get sticks."

"For what?"

"Spears," she told him.

"Hmm." He nodded off.

Delly clambered down the ladder.

When she'd gathered enough long, skinny branches, she hauled them up the tree, and stacked them in a corner of the hideawaysis.

She woke RB at the whistle. "Shhh," she whispered. They lay the blanket over Ferris Boyd, and tiptoed to the ladder.

Walking down the River Road, Delly still had fluff stuck to her teeth. Every time she got a taste, the pride started thumping again. It wouldn't stop till she told him.

"RB," she rasped.

"Huh?"

"You did good."

"Thanks, Del." He smiled, then he set his fluff-sticky hand in hers.

And they went on like that, stuck to each other with spit and sweet deliciousness.

Chapter 43

Wednesday after school, they were at the old Hennepin place again. Ferris Boyd played ball, and RB told about the time Tuba got in bed with Boomer. Boomer thought the dog was Clarice, till he kissed her and got a big, wet slobber back. "Oof oof oof," Tuba let him know she liked it.

When RB was done, he slid off the stoop and strolled over to Ferris Boyd.

"Hey," Delly hissed, "get back here."

But RB stood there, smiling. "Can I play?" he asked.

"Ferris Boyd, he doesn't know…" Delly started to explain, so she wouldn't freak out.

Instead, Ferris Boyd handed him the ball.

"Huh?" Delly muttered.

"Thanks," RB said. He set the ball over his head, and flung it as hard as he could. "Ooooof," he groaned

The ball flew a few feet, then dropped to the ground, like he'd killed it.

Ferris Boyd passed it to him again.

Again, RB committed basketball homicide.

"I'm not doing so good," he told her. He gave her the ball and headed to the stoop.

There was a smack, smack behind him. It made him stop.

Ferris Boyd was slapping her thigh.

"What the glub?" Delly murmured. She'd never heard the girl make a noise, let alone a loud one.

Ferris Boyd was staring at RB and pointing to her eye.

"I'm watching," he replied.

She spread her legs and held the ball between them. Her arms swept up over her head, heaving it into the air. It soared over the drive, and dropped through the hoop.

"Nice," RB sighed.

She passed the ball to him.

"Now me," he said. He spread his legs, and put the ball between them. Then he hurled it.

The ball went straight up. It came straight back down. RB had to jump out of the way so it wouldn't bop him.

"Oh," he said. He looked at Ferris Boyd.

She stomped the drive to show him where to stand. She pointed to her eye, then the basket.

"I'll watch the basket," he repeated.

He windmilled his arms to warm up. Then he flung the ball, like a tiny human catapult. "Oooowooof," he grunted.

It sailed through the air. It hit the rim, and passed through it.

"Holy shikes," Delly breathed.

RB was still watching the hoop. "Ferris Boyd?" he whispered, asking if it was true.

She got her pad and pen. She wrote something,

and put the paper between them.

RB took it, and his face bloomed a smile. "I want to quit with that," he told her, and went to the stoop.

"Now I got two of you playing that bawlgram game," Delly pretended to grumble. But it was something, to see him so happy.

"What's that paper say?" she asked.

He passed it to her. There were no words; just a star in the center of it. "She thinks I'm a star," he breathed, like if he said it out loud he'd be lying. He was shining, though.

Delly understood. That's how having a friend made her feel, too.

"You're the star," she rasped, wanting him to feel that way forever.

In the hideawaysis, RB didn't waste any time shimmying over to Ferris Boyd and sharing her book.

But Delly didn't worry now. She got up to go.

"Huh?" he asked.

"Getting spearheads," she answered, and went to the woods.

The forest floor was covered with limestone. If Delly banged two chunks together, small, pointy pieces broke off.

She made enough for thirty spears. When she went back, she piled them by the sticks.

Then she sat down across from those two.

She watched RB leaning on Ferris Boyd, pointing at the pages, and the girl nodding so her chin rubbed against his hair. And Delly's heart got so big, it was hammering her chest.

"RB," she rasped. Not to stop him; to let him know she was wrong.

Because Ferris Boyd had given Delly a world away from trouble, and she loved it. She'd thought RB would wreck it. Instead, he'd made it better. He filled it with his warm softness, so the hideawaysis felt like the happiest place ever.

RB glanced up at his sister.

She nodded. Without saying a word she told him, I'm glad you're here.

RB smiled so all his teeth showed.

And Delly had to turn away, before her heart busted out of her.

Chapter 44

Thursday, the Pattisons were telling tales before they even got to the stoop. On the River Road, RB started it. "Delly, remember that time Tuba snuck into the IGA?"

"Yep," she answered. "She went straight for the doughnuts."

"She used her nose to open the case," he went on, "and gobbled up all the cream-filled ones, so she was drooling white goo.

"Then Clayton Fitch spotted her. 'That dog's foaming at the mouth,' he screamed, and shot out the door. And Tuba ran after him, because she thought he was playing tag."

The Pattisons were laughing so hard, they didn't see it.

But Ferris Boyd did. She froze in the road.

They turned to her. "Ferris Boyd?" Delly asked.

She was paler than pale. Her eyes were fixed on one spot.

They followed her gaze down the drive.

The green Impala was parked in front of the garage, right where Ferris Boyd played ball.

"What's he doing here?" Delly demanded.

The girl didn't move.

The day was warm, but Delly shivered. She wasn't sure why, but she didn't want her friend to go where the man in the green Impala was. "Hey," she said, "how about we go straight to the hideawaysis?"

Ferris Boyd kept staring.

So Delly stood between the car and her friend. "Ferris Boyd, how about you come home with us?"

She saw Delly, then. She took out her pad and pen and wrote, YOU GO HOME.

"We're staying with you," Delly answered, and RB nodded.

Ferris Boyd pushed the pen hard into the paper, tracing GO HOME over and over.

"You sure?" Delly rasped.

Ferris Boyd glanced at the green Impala, and nodded. Then she slumped down the drive and into the house.

"Delly," RB started to say, "I don't want to—"

"We're not leaving," she told him. "Come on."

She led him to the ditch, and they dove in. They peaked over the edge. "We'll watch from here," she announced.

But Ferris Boyd didn't come out with her ball or the cat's bowl.

The Pattisons were concentrating so hard on the house, they didn't notice something creeping behind them. "Maow," it called.

They jumped. "Bawlgram cat," Delly hissed.

The cat cringed. It was worried, too.

"Well, shikes," Delly said. "Get over here."

The cat slid up to her.

"We're waiting for Ferris Boyd," she explained.

"Mooooowr," it cried.

Then the three of them watched. Nothing moved around that place, though; even the birds were quiet.

When the whistle blew Delly ordered, "RB, go home."

"I'm not leaving," he told her.

"If you don't go, Ma'll be scared. They'll come looking and…"

RB understood. "What do I say about you?"

"Say I'm in trouble."

"They wouldn't keep you so late."

He was right.

Delly was staring at the house, trying to come up with something, when she spotted a pale skinny girl in the upstairs window. She looked like a ghost. She put one hand against the glass.

"There she is," Delly whispered.

"Oh," RB sighed.

And she was gone

Delly turned to the cat. "You all right?"

It blinked once.

Then the two Pattisons ran, like something was

after them, all the way home.

After dinner, they lay on Delly's bed. They both had questions begging to be asked, like "Why would somebody be so scared of her dad?" and "What happened to her when she went inside?" But the only answers they could think of made their stomachs turn, and their hearts sick. So they kept quiet.

"Lights out," Clarice called, and RB shuffled to his room.

At two a.m., Delly was standing beside Clarice's bed again. "Ma," she rasped.

"Delly," Clarice murmured.

"Ma, you ever worry about somebody being in trouble?"

"Mmm," Clarice answered. Because she had, a lot.

"You ever think...you ever wonder..."

"Say it," Clarice mumbled, because sleep time was ticking away.

"You ever worry somebody's getting hurt?"

And Clarice was wide awake. She was sitting

straight up, shouting, "Who's hurt?"

Delly knew that tone: Clarice smelled trouble, and she was hunting for it. If Delly didn't throw her off the scent, Clarice'd track down the truth about her and RB's project. They'd be dead as ducks in a birddog's mouth.

So she said, "You know how on TV there's a kid getting hurt, but nobody knows because she doesn't tell?"

Clarice had her arms crossed. "Mm-hmm."

"Well, how would you know if somebody's getting hurt when she doesn't say anything?"

"Is this about something on TV?" Clarice demanded.

"I saw something," was Delly's almost-true answer.

Clarice calmed down. "Delly, TV isn't real."

"But I need to know," she insisted.

Clarice lay back again. "Well," she said, "if somebody was getting injured, there might be marks. There are ways to hurt people without it showing, though."

Delly was listening.

"Maybe she'd seem sad. Maybe, if she had a friend, she'd tell her, or give her hints."

"Like what?" Delly wondered.

Clarice was quiet for a minute. "I don't know," she said.

Then Clarice's voice was steel, so sharp it would cut through any untruth, "Delly, is somebody hurting you, or one of your brothers or sisters?"

"No, Ma," she told her.

Clarice let out a sigh. After a while, her breaths got farther and farther apart.

"Ma," Delly whispered, "can I?"

Clarice lifted the covers.

Delly crawled in. She wouldn't cuddle up to Clarice, because she wasn't a baby. But she kept one arm against her mother, the warm softness of Clarice telling her she wasn't alone.

Chapter 45

Friday morning, Delly and RB were waiting at the back door to the school.

"There." Delly pointed.

They watched her shuffle toward them. She was still pale and skinny. She still hunched over.

"She's okay?" RB asked, and they both nodded, because they wanted it to be true.

When she got to the door, they fell in on either side of her. They walked her to her desk, then stood beside her like sentries.

"Mr. Pattison," Lionel Terwilliger announced, "Your presence is required elsewhere." So RB had to go.

"See you later, Ferris Boyd," he said softly.

When he was gone, Delly leaned over. "You all right?" she whispered.

Ferris Boyd just sat there, but Delly waited. After a long time, her head dropped to her chest.

Like a nod, Delly thought. Or giving up.

All day, Delly watched her friend from her seat. At recess, she left Alaska for the tree next to Ferris Boyd's. The creatures stayed close, too.

It was a long, slow walk to the old Hennepin place.

When they got to the drive they saw it: No green Impala.

Delly let out a big breath, like she'd been holding it all day. "It'll be okay." She sighed.

And it was. Almost.

The cat came. They told stories. Ferris Boyd and RB played ball.

But everywhere they went, a shadow followed them. It cast a gloom over every happiness. It was shaped like the man in the green Impala.

At the hideawaysis, Delly took out some string and Boomer's pocket knife. She cut a groove in the end of each stick, slipped a piece of limestone in, then tied it tight.

"Those are nice spears." RB touched the tip of one.

"For invaders," she told him.

She set them standing around the rails, like soldiers. "Nothing can hurt us here," she breathed.

But all the while Delly was working, a question pestered her: What if the enemy's not at the hideawaysis? it asked.

She was too busy to answer.

When the whistle blew, she kneeled down beside her friend. "Okay, Ferris Boyd, you got rocks and spears. There's the blanket, food, and the rope for quick escapes. You going to be all right?"

Ferris Boyd gazed at all her friend had done. She looked into Delly's eyes; they were full of wanting her to be safe. And she nodded.

Then they left her, surrounded by every protection Delly knew how to give.

Chapter 46

Saturday was the first ever Delly Day. "Happy Hallelujah!" she hollered when she woke up. She galloped downstairs, smiling so big you could see her tonsils.

After breakfast, Clarice asked her, "Well, Delly, what do you want to do?"

But Delly didn't know how to ask for what she wanted most. So she said, "Can we get doughnuts?"

"Sure," Clarice told her, and they headed out the door.

At the IGA, Clarice got a bag. "How many do you want?"

Delly didn't need a dozen, because she had Clarice, but two seemed too few. "Six," she decided, and picked them.

"Hey, Norma," Clarice greeted her at the checkout.

"Hey, Clarice. What you up to?" Norma replied.

"Celebrating." She smiled at Delly. "No trouble, for a month."

Delly waited for Norma to snort, or snicker. Instead she stood there thinking, It had been a long time since she'd kicked Delly out for spitting, or writing nocuss words on the windows. "Huh," she said.

Outside, Clarice asked, "What do you want to do next?"

"Could we go to the river?"

So they did. They sat on the bank and watched the water, just the two of them.

Delly opened up the doughnuts. She picked a chocolate-iced chocolate-filled chocolate one, and passed the bag to Clarice. She was about to load her mouth with lusciousness, when her mom stopped her.

"Let's have a toast." Clarice raised her doughnut

in the air. "To Delly," she said, and took a bite. "Now you eat it," she told her.

But Delly couldn't move. Clarice toasting her made her insides so warm and mushy, her whole body got floppy. Her floppy fingers dropped the doughnut in her lap.

Delly didn't mind. Because suddenly the whole world was a doughnut: Sweet, beautiful, and delicious. And she was the floppy cream filling. She hummed the song of gooey, goopy happiness, "Hmmmm."

When Clarice was done with her doughnut, she turned to Delly. "You ready to go home?"

Just like that, all the deliciousness disappeared. Even on a Dellyday, Clarice had something else to do.

"Okay," she started to mumble. Till the question paper pinched her.

Still, she could only whisper it, she wanted it so much. "Ma, can we stay for a while?"

Clarice heard the wanting in that tiny whisper. "Sure," she said.

The sweet wonderfulness surrounded Delly again. She rolled back onto the bank, smiling.

Clarice lay down beside her.

They stayed like that for a long time.

Finally, Delly had what she wanted most. So she said, "Want to go home?"

"You sure?" Clarice asked.

"Sure," she answered. Because she knew, someday soon, she'd have it again.

Chapter 47

Every week, Brud Kinney and Ferris Boyd's games got longer and longer, because Brud kept thinking of animals with longer and longer names. Plus he was getting better.

But there was never enough basketball for Brud.

Sunday morning, he walked down the drive to the old Hennepin place and held up his pad.

T-Y-R-R-A-N-A-S-A-U-R-U-S R-E-X, it read, *NO TOUCH*.

The boy read it while Brud held his breath. Then he nodded.

The happiness was going to shoot Brud like a rocket into outer space. His feet were already blasting off. So right there, in front of the boy, he hollered, A-a-a-ll right!"

And Ferris Boyd didn't flinch, or make fun. She just waited for him to come back to earth.

Then they played. The game went on and on, like heaven's supposed to. Ferris Boyd beat him, but not by much.

After, they were worn out. They both went to the stoop. They lay back on it, stinking with sweat.

Even if he didn't have the stutter, there wasn't much Brud wanted to say. He didn't need to chat, "Nice day", or talk about his new sneakers.

But there was something that mattered more than anything to Brud. He'd never told it to anybody. He wanted his friend to know.

So he wrote it: I want to play like nothing nobody's ever seen, only better.

The boy read it. He stared at the sky for a while. Then he wrote, YOU WILL.

Brud turned to his friend to see if he was making fun, or feeling sorry.

The boy's eyes were steady and sure. He meant it.

Then Brud didn't smile, or nod, or write anything. It was all too small for how he felt. He just stared at the sky, thinking, Thanks.

Chapter 48

Finally, it was the date Delly Pattison waited all year for: The last day of school. But Delly wasn't "Yahoo!"ing; she was worried. "Summer's vacation from school. And people, too, if you want," she fretted.

So she didn't ask as they walked out the River Road, with RB singing, "No more school, no more schoo-oo-ool." She didn't ask during basketball, even though the paper was pinching her. She didn't get it out till it was two minutes to the whistle.

"Ferris Boyd, I got a question," she said, and the rasp was rough. "On Monday, there's no school—"

RB started singing again, "No more schoo-oo—"

"Quit it," she commanded.

"So we won't be walking out here together. We got chores in the morning, but we could...in the afternoon... if you want...." It was too hard; Delly couldn't finish.

But the paper was pinching her a purple herman. It was going to make her ask.

"Bawlgrammit," she muttered. Then she took a big breath and pushed it out. "You want us to come here and hang out with you?"

Now, there were about ten questions in those ten words, like, "Are we really friends, even outside of school?" and "Could you stand seeing more of us?" For every one of them, a "No" would hurt horribadibly.

Ferris Boyd stared into the green. She took out her pad and pen.

Delly felt sick, knowing the answer needed more than a nod. She had to make herself read it.

In big, dark letters it said, YES.

"All right then." Delly grinned so her cheeks puffed up like peaches.

"Yay," RB cheered. He started dancing around the hideawaysis. "Yay, yay, yay."

Then he stopped. "What about Gal?" he worried, because she was supposed to be watching them.

"I got that covered," Delly told him.

He went back to dancing.

The whistle blew.

At the ladder, Delly said it smiling, "See you Monday, Ferris Boyd." Because now they weren't just after-school friends. They were summer friends; they were every-bawlgram-day friends.

And Ferris Boyd nodded.

After dinner, Delly went to Galveston's room. She knocked on the door.

"What?" Gal hollered.

"Can I come in?"

Gal waited a while before she said, "Okay." That made Delly mad; but she had questions for her sister, not a fight.

Galveston was on her bed with a book.

"Gal," Delly began.

"Huh."

"You know how you're watching me and RB this summer?"

"Babysitting you. Yeah," she said. It was just mean calling it that, but Delly let it slide.

"You know how you got to be with us all day, and take us every place you go?"

Galveston groaned.

"What if you didn't have to be with us so much? And you'd get paid."

"Go on," she said.

"Me and RB will do our chores in the morning, then we'll take off for the afternoon," Delly explained. "We'll be home before Ma, and we'll act like we were with you the whole time."

"And where are you going to be?" Gal demanded.

"At the old Hennepin place."

"Doing what?"

"Hanging around, with my friend."

It was too good to believe, and it was too good to say "No" to. Gal started grilling her. "You going to the river?"

"Nope."

"Taking people's stuff?"

"Nope."

"Fighting? Setting off firecrackers?"

"Nope."

Galveston paused. If it worked, it'd be heaven. If something went wrong, there'd be the flames of Clarice's fury. "What if something bad happens? What if you get in trouble while I'm supposed to be watching you?"

"I'll say we snuck out on you. I'll say it was me," Delly replied.

Gal squinted at her. "Swear on it."

"Cross my heart or cover me with cow chips," she promised.

"Okay." Gal went back to her book, letting Delly know they were done.

But Delly had more. "What's Ma paying you to watch us?"

"Three dollars an hour."

"How about splitting it with us?" she suggested.

Galveston laughed out loud.

"Gal," Delly said, "RB tells Ma everything. I bet some money would help keep him quiet."

Gal heard what she was meaning. "Two dollars a day," she offered.

"A dollar an hour," Delly countered.

Gal chewed on that. "Okay, but if you mess up I get all of it."

"Deal," Delly told her.

And that's how the youngest Pattisons came into some extra money that summer.

Chapter 49

After that, the Pattisons were at the old Hennepin place every weekday by noon, bringing lunch, good times, and armaments.

With the money they got from Galveston, they bought fluff, chocolate bars, and a box of graham crackers.

"First, you spread the fluff on a cracker. Next comes the chocolate. Then you slap a cracker on top." Delly demonstrated. "Fantabulous," she declared, spitting cracker dust.

"S'more, please, s'more please," RB sang as his belly got big with them.

Ferris Boyd just closed her eyes while she

chewed and chewed.

Delly made slingshots for each of them. "Ready, aim, blast 'em," she hollered, as she taught those two how to shoot.

She got eggs, and left them in the sun.

"Won't they go bad?" RB asked.

Her eyes sparkled as she said, "They're stink bombs. You hit somebody with one, and the stench'll knock him out."

She brought a shovel, and dug holes in the ground around the hideawaysis. She covered them with evergreen branches. Then she showed Ferris Boyd and RB where they were. "Traps, for intruders," she warned them.

It took over a month to get the jobs done. Delly didn't mind. She was with her friend, with no school and no Novello to bother them. No green Impala, either.

Sometimes, she thought about asking, "Ferris Boyd, where's your dad?" Because even though Boomer and Clarice were gone a lot, there was always somebody around to watch Delly and RB. Nobody was watching Ferris Boyd.

But she couldn't say it, as if the words might bring the green Impala back. She wouldn't risk ruining the happiness.

And in June, she got another Delly Day.

Clarice borrowed a canoe, but she wouldn't go down the river; they took it to the lake instead.

They went in the morning, before everybody else got up. They paddled around for a while, and it was so peaceful Delly almost fell asleep again.

Till something blew up beside them. Smack, it hit the water, then splash. Smack, splash. The water kept exploding, like they were in a mine field.

"Grenades!" Delly screamed. "Ma, get down!"

Clarice was laughing. "That's the carp," she explained. "They rest in the shallows. We're waking them up."

"Oh." She calmed down.

They cruised to the middle of the lake and Clarice got breakfast out—egg sandwiches and doughnuts. And Delly was so happy, all she could do was smile.

They watched the deer come down to the water

to drink. "Ma," Delly whispered and pointed, and Clarice nodded. Then they stayed still for a long time.

"This is the best summer ever," Delly breathed to the wind and the sun and the water. "Nothing can wreck it."

Brud Kinney was having the best summer, too.

Weekdays, he worked on his grandparents' farm, and that was all right.

But on Sundays, he was with his friend. He didn't go to the park anymore; he stayed at Ferris Boyd's all day.

One Sunday at the end of June, after they played R-H-I-N-O-C-E-R-O-S for the third time, he was so happy he had to write it, *This is the best summer ever.*

Ferris Boyd's eyes smiled.

Nothing can wreck it, Brud wrote surely.

Ferris Boyd closed her eyes, as if she was wishing the words would be true.

But Brud was wrong.

They all were.

Chapter 50

It was July. It was Sunday. For the Pattisons, that meant church. But this Sunday, there wasn't just church in the morning. "We got church the whole bawlgram day," Delly griped. Because after the sermon, there was a picnic for everybody at the park outside of town.

"Yay," RB cheered when Clarice said, "We're going."

So Delly set him straight. "A church picnic's not like a real one," she told him. "There's no swimming in your underwear, or mudball fights. You just play baby games and talk to old people."

RB looked like he might cry, so she added,

"They got good food, though."

After the service, they all got in the van. Delly took a window seat.

"Move over," Galveston ordered.

"I feel sick," Delly replied. "You want me to throw up on you?"

So Gal climbed in behind her, and the questions won again.

As they drove down the River Road, RB yelled, "Hey Delly, we're going by—," but she "Shhhh"-ed him silent.

Then she turned to the window, because she wanted to see if Ferris Boyd and that cat were outside.

She spotted the cat on the stoop. And there was Ferris Boyd, playing ball in the drive.

But she wasn't alone. Somebody was with Delly's friend.

The somebody turned to the road, smiling. The sun shone on his two front teeth so they glowed.

"That's Brud Kinney," RB said, like it was a happy thing.

Delly just kept turning in her seat, watching those two together. "What the glub?" she mumbled.

"What are you griping about?" Galveston asked.

"Nothing," she muttered. But it didn't feel like nothing. It felt like something. Something bad.

Suddenly, Delly had all kinds of questions. For herself. Questions like, How long's he been going out there? Are they friends? How much fun are they having? And the only answer she had was, I don't know, because my friend doesn't tell me anything. Delly hadn't felt this bad in a long time.

At the picnic, Clarice sat her between Mabel Silcox and Angel Grace Pincher. While the two old ladies chatted about prunes and support hose, the questions wouldn't leave Delly alone. How long does he stay out there? they asked. Did she show him the hideawaysis?

After lunch, there were games. Clarice made Delly and Galveston do the three-legged race together. "So you work as a team," she told them. Gal's legs ended at Delly's eyeballs, though, so they kept falling over each other.

Delly won the seed-spitting contest without even trying. They let her pick a prize, but all they had were socks and mittens the church ladies had knitted. "Chizzle," she grumbled.

She sat on a bench, and the questions followed her. Does she like him better? they wondered. Now that she's got him, will she get rid of me?

RB sat beside her. "You got socks!" he exclaimed, like they'd given her a chocolate cake.

"Take them," she said.

"I got socks, I got socks," he sang.

Delly wasn't getting any answers on her own, so she asked RB. "How come Ferris Boyd didn't let us know she's friends with Brud Kinney?"

"Maybe she didn't think we'd care," he answered

"I don't care," she huffed.

Instead of saying, "Yes you do," RB told her, "Maybe because they play basketball and you hate that game."

She chewed on that for a bit; it could be true. Then she rasped, "RB, do you think Ferris Boyd likes us?"

"She likes us a lot." He said it so surely, she believed it. Almost.

"Because she doesn't tell us anything," she argued.

He laughed. "Delly, she doesn't talk."

"Bawlgrammit, RB," she shouted. "I mean she doesn't let us know stuff."

'We know about the hideawaysis, and that she loves basketball and animals."

Delly knew all that was a big deal. "But... about her."

"She's just sad," he replied.

"Huh," she said, because she knew that was true. Now she had more questions, though, like, Does sad make you stop talking? And, Does sad keep secrets?

Clarice came by, herding her horde to the van. "Delly, you sit up front with me," she decided.

They rode for a while before Delly asked, "Ma?"

"Yep."

The rasp was so soft, Clarice could hardly hear her. "If you got a friend, then she gets another friend, do you get less friend?"

Clarice thought about it. "I don't know about friends; I know about kids. Will that do?"

Delly shrugged.

So Clarice told her, "After I married your dad, we had Dallas. He was the only one, and I loved him a lot.

"Then Tallahassee came along, and I had less time for Dallas, but I loved him more because we were a family.

"It was the same with Montana, Gal, you, and RB. I got less time for anybody, I know it Delly. But I got more love for everybody. More than I knew I had in me." Clarice's voice cracked. "That make sense?"

"Maybe," she answered. Because Delly liked everybody more since she had Ferris Boyd.

Everybody except Brud Kinney.

Chapter 51

Monday, Delly waited till they were at the hide-awaysis to say, "Shikes! I left my bag at the bottom of the tree. RB, will you get it?"

He was already settled in beside Ferris Boyd; he didn't want to go.

"Please?" she asked. "The sandwiches are in it. Plus I brought cookies."

And he couldn't say "No" to that.

When he was out of earshot, Delly started. "Hey Ferris Boyd, I don't have a question for this; I just got to say it."

The girl's eyes came to her.

She said it quick, so it wouldn't hurt so much.

"I didn't have friends for a long time before you. Sometimes I think you might quit being my friend, because everybody else did. So, if you got other friends, that's all right."

Delly couldn't look at her for the last part. "Just keep being my friend, okay?"

Ferris Boyd gazed into the green. She took out her pad and pen, then passed the note to Delly. OK, it read.

Delly leaned back against the rail, and breathed out all the worry that had been weighing on her. "All right then." She and Ferris Boyd were okay.

Brud Kinney, however, was a different matter.

Chapter 32

Tuesday after supper, RB and Delly had nothing to do.

"Want to make worm muffins?" he asked her.

"Nah."

"Want to listen to Gal talking to her boyfriend on the phone?"

"No," she told him, because that was just weird. "How much money we got?" she asked.

"Lots."

"Let's go get some doughnuts."

They got two triple chocolates. They sat in front of the IGA eating them, not spitting once.

And didn't Brud Kinney ride up on his bike,

because his mother sent him for milk.

Before Sunday, Delly'd always liked Brud. She liked his stutter and his fake teeth. But now she had something she wanted him to know. "Hey, Brud Kinney," she called.

Brud Kinney liked Delly, too. He liked her voice, and how she took on Novello. But he knew about her fighting. He waved from far away.

"Hold on," she said, as he walked toward the door.

So he did.

"I saw you playing ball with Ferris Boyd. You go out there every Sunday?" she wondered.

Brud nodded, then he watched her. He wanted to see if a fight was headed his way before it hit him.

"Well, she's my friend, too," Delly told him.

Brud's eyes got big, like she'd punched him. "Wh-wh-who?" he said.

"Ferris Boyd," she announced. "She's my friend. First."

Brud's head felt funny, as if a piece of surest knowing was getting sucked out of it. "H-h-he's not—"

"Yes she is," Delly declared. "She's my best friend."

He saw the sureness in her face, and he knew it was true. And just like that, there was a giant hole in Brud's brain where everything he knew about Ferris Boyd had been.

Delly saw his surprise. That's all right, she thought; now he knows where he stands. She nodded and turned toward the lot.

Brud stumbled into the store.

After he was gone, RB said, "Delly, how come Brud called Ferris Boyd 'He'?"

She thought about it. "Stutter," she decided.

But while they walked home, Delly remembered the shock on Brud's face when she told him, "She." Maybe he'd made the same mistake about Ferris Boyd that Delly had, but nobody'd corrected him. Till today.

"Chizzle," she muttered.

"Huh?" RB asked.

"Nothing," she said, hoping that was true.

Back at the IGA, Brud couldn't remember what he'd come for. He stood in the aisle thinking, Ferris Boyd, he's a … she.

The thoughts rolled out from there: I've been playing with a girl. I've been writing notes to a girl. I've been wishing more than anything to be like… her.

It wasn't that Brud thought a girl couldn't play ball. But he thought he had a friend, a best one, a boy. He was wrong about all of it.

"You all right?" Norma asked.

"Huh?" he mumbled, and walked out the door to his bike.

Every other time he'd passed the old Hennepin place, Brud had searched for the boy, hoping to see his friend. Now he pedaled hard and stared ahead, like the place wasn't there.

At home, his mother asked, "Where's the milk?"

He checked his hands, as if they might be holding it.

"There's nothing," she told him.

And Brud nodded: He'd gone to the store having a friend; now he had nothing.

Sunday, Brud Kinney did not get up early.

When he finally went to town, he didn't ride his bike down the River Road. He went up the hill near his house, along the highway, and back down to River Bluffs.

"Well, look who's here," Novello sneered.

Brud played ball, but he was bad. Every time he shot or dribbled he'd think, Ferris Boyd, my...that girl taught me this. It messed him up.

"You all right?" Gwennie asked.

Brud nodded, because nothing was true.

He played at the park all day. He went home the long way again.

That night in bed, Brud couldn't sleep for missing his friend.

"Get over it," his head said. "It wasn't real anyway."

But the rest of him didn't listen; it just kept missing.

Chapter 53

Sunday was another Delly Day. This time, she got Boomer.

"Where do you want to go?" he asked her.

"Hickory Corners," she answered, because they had ice cream. And there was something she needed to see. "Can we drive out the River Road?"

"Sure," he said.

As they came to the old Hennepin place, Ferris Boyd was standing in the drive bouncing her ball, ping, ping, ping, like a call. She was looking down the road for something that should be coming.

"No Brud Kinney," Delly snickered.

But as they passed, she saw the loneliness on her

friend's face. "Huh," she murmured.

At the ice cream shop, they both got chocolate with chocolate sauce and chocolate sprinkles. It was so delicious they couldn't speak.

When they were done, though, Boomer said, "Well, Delly, three months of no trouble. I didn't think it would happen."

That hurt, hearing he hadn't believed she could do it.

But he went on. "I was like you: I was in so much trouble when I was little. It didn't stop till I was a lot older."

"You were never this little," she told him

"Yes, I was."

"You were never in this much trouble."

"More," he said. "My Ma cried all the time." His head went down.

"How come you didn't stop?" she asked.

"Didn't know how. My dad tried to knock it out of me. They sent me away to school. Nothing worked."The shame still weighed so heavy on him, he hunched over.

Delly knew that heaviness. She tried to lift some of it off him. "You never hit me," she said.

"I couldn't hurt you."

"And you're not in trouble now," she told him.

"I met your Ma. She thought I was all right, and that helped."

Delly nodded. She knew what that could do.

"Then we had you kids, and I didn't want you to be ashamed of me."

"I'm never ashamed of you," she whispered.

"I'm glad," he said. "Del." He looked at her now. "You're doing good. You're doing what I couldn't do."

Delly gazed at her dad, who was big and a boy and nothing like her. But in a way they were the same. Because they both knew what it felt like to be bad, and to think that's what you'd be forever. They both knew how good it was to be wrong about that.

"Know what else works for trouble?" she told him. "Counting."

"Yeah?"

"And questions. You got to ask questions."

"I'll try that," he agreed. "Where else do you want to go?"

"Let's go home," she said, because she had something to check on.

Ferris Boyd was still in the drive when they drove by. She wasn't bouncing the ball anymore. She was just staring out the River Road, toward Brud Kinney's place. The cat was circling, bumping her with its body.

Delly'd never seen anything so lonely.

As the van passed, the cat sighted Delly. "Maoh," it cried out, You did this.

"Shikes," she muttered, scrunching down in her seat.

"What?" Boomer wondered.

"Nothing," she answered; but she knew it wasn't.

Chapter 54

Monday, Ferris Boyd was different.

There was always a sadness in her. But if it was usually a couple of cups full, now it was gallons, and it poured out of her all the time.

She quit playing ball early, and Delly didn't cheer because she knew it wasn't good.

At the hideawaysis, she had her book, but mostly she gazed out toward Kinney's. Her eyes were missing and hurting, like Delly would feel if her friend wasn't around anymore.

So she told her, "You know, Ferris Boyd, in summer people go away on vacation. They don't tell their friends; they just go."

That seemed to help.

And Ferris Boyd got better as the week went on. She was best on Friday, wanting to practice.

She's hoping he's coming, Delly thought.

Delly was, too. Because it wasn't better without Brud Kinney.

Sunday was scorching hot. After church and changing clothes, Delly got her money and went to the kitchen.

"Ma, can I go watch some basketball?" she asked.

Clarice looked at her suspiciously. "You hate that game," she said.

That stumped Delly.

Then RB was beside her. "She's taking me," he announced. "I love basketball."

"All right," Clarice agreed.

At the corner Delly tried to shame him, "Is that all you do—watch me and follow me around?"

It didn't work. "Yep." He smiled.

"Jiminy fipes," she muttered, but she knew he'd saved her.

"I got something to check on," she told him. "Don't mess me up."

"I know," he answered.

When they got to the River Road, they went into the ditch. "Shhh," she warned him.

"I know," he whispered.

Across from the drive, she peaked over the edge. There was Ferris Boyd, sitting on the stoop with the ball in her lap. She was staring up the road, looking lonelier than the week before. The cat was wrapped around her legs like a comfort.

"Bawldoublegrammit," she rasped. "Come on."

They sauntered down the drive as if they were out for a Sunday stroll. "Ferris Boyd," Delly exclaimed, like it was a surprise to see her.

She turned to them, her eyes two pitchers of sadness. Then she went back to watching for him.

The Pattisons sat on either side of her. "Ferris Boyd," Delly asked, "you want me to play ball with you?" because she would do it to help her friend.

She shook her head.

So the three of them stared up the road, like

they were waiting for a parade that was way past due.

By noon, it was so hot they were dripping sweat from just sitting.

The cat went into the woods.

Delly stood up. "I can't take this heat anymore. Let's go."

"Where are we going?" RB wondered.

"To get refreezerated," she told him, and they walked up the drive.

Ferris Boyd stayed on the stoop.

"Ferris Boyd," Delly called, "come with us. Please?"

Maybe it was the heat. Or maybe she knew Delly was trying to help. Whatever it was, Ferris Boyd glanced up the River Road one more time, then slumped to them.

They dragged themselves into town. By the time they got to the IGA, they were so wet with sweat they looked like they'd showered.

"Here," Delly ordered, and led them inside.

The store was air-conditioned. "Ahhh," RB said.

Ferris Boyd closed her eyes.

"This way," Delly directed.

They went to the back of the store, to the wall of frozen foods. Behind the glass doors was Antarctica. Delly opened one, and a cloud of cold came out of it. "Shikes," she sighed.

"Get your own," she told the other two; so they did.

"Mmmmm," RB hummed. Ferris Boyd stood so close to hers, she almost fell in.

The three of them were standing with their eyes closed, pretending they were in a snow storm. So they didn't see Clayton Fitch come down the aisle.

"You got those Pattisons climbing into your coolers," he told Norma at the checkout.

She barreled to the back of the store. "You looking for something?" she shouted.

They were so surprised, they slammed their doors.

"Buy something or get out," she barked, and stomped away.

"Come on," Delly told them.

They walked over to the ice cream. There were tubs, cartons, and tiny containers filled with frozen heaven.

"What do you want?" she asked them.

They thought about getting pints, so they could each have their own. "Not big enough," Delly decided.

"What about this?" RB picked up the family size.

"Hmm." Delly admired his ambitiousness. "But it'll melt before we're done," she said sadly.

"We'll share a half-gallon." She settled it. "If we want more, we'll get another."

They chose it together: Chocolate with chocolate chunks and a fudge ribbon running through it. On their way to the checkout, Delly picked up a box of plastic spoons.

"What about napkins?" RB wondered.

She tugged at the bottom of her shirt and RB understood—it was for wiping.

At the register, Delly pulled out a wad of money while Ferris Boyd searched her pockets. "We got it," Delly told her. "Babysitting money." She grinned.

Then she asked, "Hey, Norma, can we eat this on the sidewalk?"

Now, Norma had already planned it out: She was going to wait till those Pattisons sat on her walk to holler, "Move along!" She didn't know what to do with Delly asking permission. "All right," she grumbled.

"Don't let it melt," Delly told them as she opened the ice cream. They ate it fast.

When they were done, Ferris Boyd was blue. RB was shaking from his insides being frozen.

"You want another one?" Delly asked.

"Maybe later," he replied, because his stomach was cramping up.

They lay down on the walk, and let the sun unfreeze them.

Delly stared at the sky. "I got over three months of no trouble," she rasped. She didn't say, "Because of the counting, and the questions." But she turned her head to RB, then Ferris Boyd, letting them know, Thanks.

And they nodded, as if they heard her.

"We're like the three musketeers," she said. "We're the three chumbudions."

The sound of it made her smile. RB, too. Even Ferris Boyd's mouth turned up the tiniest bit.

Then RB said, "Delly, I need a drink. Can we buy some water?"

"We're not paying for water," she told him. "We'll go to the park."

And that's how they ended up over by the basketball court—for the free water fountain.

Chapter 55

Brud, Novello, and the others had been playing ball for a while, but it was too hot. They turned red, then got dizzy with it. Tater almost passed out.

So they lay down in the shade, trying to cool off. That's why the three chumbudions didn't spot them.

Danny Novello had been without Delly all summer, and his heart ached with her absence. He heard the rasp that was his heart's favorite sound, and it started pounding.

"Get away, you're giving me heat stroke." He shoved Tater and sat up.

And he saw, across the park, those copper curls

bouncing. He raced, with his basketball and his cruel love, toward her.

The three chumbudions were done drinking. They were headed back to the IGA for another half-gallon. Delly didn't notice Novello till he was in front of her.

"What the glub?" she muttered.

"Hey Smelly," he greeted her, "long time no stink."

Delly had no time for Novello's nastiness; she side-stepped him.

He blocked her.

She tried again, but he was right there, keeping her in the heat and away from ice cream. The mad flamed up inside her. Still, she asked, "Will you please get out of my way?"

"No," he answered.

"Leave her alone," RB hollered.

"Back off, Tiny Tim," he sneered.

That hurt RB. Delly saw it, and the mad went to high heat. "What do you want?" she shouted.

He smirked. "Play me. Basketball. If you win,

you can go. If I win, you got to do what I want." He puckered up, revealing his plan.

"I'd rather eat cow patties," she croaked.

It was cruel poetry, the way she talked. It made him love her more. "I can stay here forever," he said.

She looked into his eyes, and knew it was true. And she'd run out of questions except, "One knuckle sandwich or two?"

Delly considered her options: She could play him, but she'd lose. She could run, but they'd call her "Chicken" and she couldn't live with that. Or she could fight him.

The mad liked that idea, a lot.

"If I fight, I'll lose everything," she breathed. "What am I going to do?"

Novello decided it. He dropped the ball and picked up RB. "Me or the munchkin?" he demanded.

"Put me down!" RB wailed.

Delly's fists were up. "I'm going to pound you into the pavement," she snarled.

"Don't!" RB yelled. "Remember Delly Days."

The fight didn't care about Delly Days. Her

right fist cocked back behind her head. "You're going down," she growled.

Novello smirked, knowing his true love would be touching him soon.

Instead two pale, skinny hands slapped each other, SMACK SMACK SMACK between them.

"What the...?" Novello exclaimed. They all turned to the smacker.

Ferris Boyd's eyes were wild, like she wanted to run. But there was something else in them, too; something strong.

"What do you want?" Novello snapped.

She picked up the basketball. She pointed at him, then herself.

"No, Ferris Boyd," Delly rasped.

But Novello remembered the game in gym class. "You want to play for Smelly?" He laughed.

Ferris Boyd nodded. Then she turned to her friend. Delly could almost hear her, If you fight, it's over. I don't want to lose you.

"Okay," Delly whispered.

"Yes!" Novello yelped. "Let's play." He smacked

his lips, like a lion about to gobble up a dumb little lamb.

Ferris Boyd took out her pad. She held it up to him.

"You want to play H-O-R-S-E?" He was laughing hard. "That's a baby game."

She pointed to the paper.

"Fine," he jeered.

She flipped the page.

"No touch," he read. "You want me to give you the

H-O-R-S, too?"

She shook her head.

"If she wins," RB piped up, "you leave all of us alone. Forever."

"She won't win," he scoffed.

"That's the deal," RB insisted.

"Whatever," Novello said. "Let's go."

They walked across the park. Ferris Boyd's eyes were blue steel.

Chapter 56

The others were still lying on the grass when Novello and Ferris Boyd stepped onto the court.

"What are you doing?" Tater asked.

"Stay out of the way," Novello warned him. "I got a game to win."

They all sat up.

When Brud spotted Ferris Boyd, he dropped his head so she wouldn't see him. But the girl only saw the basket.

"What are you playing for?" Tater asked.

Novello pointed at Delly. "Big stink in a small package."

He held the ball out. As Ferris Boyd reached for

it, he yanked it away. "Psyche," he said, and shot it at the basket. It banged against the backboard and went through the net.

"That's how it's done, fans," he told the crowd.

Ferris Boyd had the ball. She stood on the same spot, staring at the hoop.

Now, most of those kids had been in the gym when Ferris Boyd lost the game for Delly. They sat there, waiting for her to do nothing, just like that day.

Instead, they saw what happened when the girl got a ball in her hands. She bounced it like it belonged to her. She brought it to her chest, then sent it to the basket. There was no bang or clang; just the swish of perfection.

"Wow," was all Tater could say.

"Lucky," Novello sniffed, but they saw the fear in his eyes.

He took the ball way out, farther than any pale, skinny girl could shoot from, and he flung it. It smacked the backboard and ricocheted far away from the basket. "What?" he shouted, and let it go, as if it wasn't his.

Ferris Boyd got the ball. She took it to where he'd stood.

Every eye watched her; even Brud's.

She bounced it twice. She crouched down and cocked her arms over her head. Then she sprang into the air and set the ball soaring. It flew with invisible wings to the basket. It dropped down through the net like it was home.

"Ahhh," the crowd sighed, because it was beautiful.

"Whatever," Novello snorted.

He brought the ball back to the spot he'd thought would defeat her. Now he was the one who had to make the shot.

He pounded the ball against the pavement. "Grrr," he grunted as he hurled it at the hoop.

"Oooh," the others murmured when he missed.

Then Ferris Boyd got it, and they held their breaths. She kept shooting from that same spot. "Ohhh," they breathed as she swished it. They didn't know a kid could play like that.

It wasn't long till Novello had H-O-R-S. For his final shot, he set the ball over his head, as if he'd try one more time.

Then he turned and whipped it, straight at Delly. "This doesn't count!" he screamed.

"Bawlgrammit!" Delly shouted as she ducked. "You made a deal. They saw it." She pointed at the others.

Ferris Boyd's head jerked around. She'd been so focused on the game, she hadn't paid attention to the crowd. Now she scanned their faces. Till she came to Brud's.

Then the weeks of wondering were in her eyes. Brud could almost hear her, Where have you been? What happened? I missed you.

Even in his head, Brud couldn't talk right. I thought... You're not..., his brain stammered.

But Novello wasn't finished. "It doesn't count, because she can't play." He pointed at Ferris Boyd. "You have to be a boy or a girl to play this game, and SHE IS AN IT!" he shrieked.

Ferris Boyd's body buckled like he'd punched

her. But her eyes stayed with Brud, asking, Is it true?

Brud Kinney didn't have to speak. He turned away, telling her, Yes.

Ferris Boyd's head dropped to her chest. Then she ran—across the court, out of the park, and disappeared.

"I win after all," Novello snickered.

Delly walked toward him, fists at her sides.

She wasn't yelling; she wasn't mad. She was a bomb of fury, tick ticking to detonation. In a few seconds, she would explode on him.

"Delly, don't fight," RB pleaded.

Novello started stepping backwards. "What do you want, Smelly...I mean Delly?"

She kept walking. She brought her index finger up to eye level and sighted him. Soon, he would be Dellydebris.

RB flung himself on her. "We have to find Ferris Boyd," he hollered.

He slowed her, but he couldn't stop her. Nothing could prevent the annihilation of Novello.

Except Brud Kinney. He planted himself in front of her.

"What the glub," she growled.

Brud bent down so his eyes were even with hers. His mouth was moving, but she couldn't hear him over the tick, ticking.

So he shouted it, with no stutter, "Go help Ferris Boyd!"

Through the fury, it came to her: Her friend needed her. Now. Novello's extermination would have to wait.

She glanced down and saw RB hanging on her. "We got to find Ferris Boyd," she said.

"I know," he said back.

"Then get off me."

So he did.

But the fury was not finished. She turned to Novello. "You!" she roared, and the air shook with it. It sent him stumbling.

Then Delly and RB were running, across the park, over the bridge, and out the River Road.

It took a minute before Novello could speak. "Freaks," he sniped. He glanced at the crowd, expecting agreement. No one would look at him.

Except Brud Kinney. "Take it back," he ordered.

"What did you say?" Novello jeered.

Brud could feel everybody's eyes on him. "T-t-take it b-b-back."

Novello laughed. "Or what? Wh-wh-what are you g-going to d-d-do?"

And Brud knew. "I'm d-d-done."

"Then you're done," Novello told him.

Brud picked up his ball, and went to his bike.

"Bye bye, b-b-baby." Novello waved as he rode away. He turned to the rest of them. "What a loser." He waited for them to laugh.

Without a word, Gwennie got up and walked away. The others followed.

"Where do you think you're going?" Novello sniped.

No one answered.

"Losers," he muttered, to only himself.

Chapter 57

They found her at the hideawaysis. She was curled up in her corner, rocking back and forth, back and forth with her eyes closed.

She'd written IT in the wood all around her. Big ITs, small ITs, they sneered and screamed at her.

The cat was watching her, crying, "Maoh."

For a moment the Pattisons stood there, staring.

"Oh," RB sighed, and he was scared.

"Ferris Boyd," Delly hollered, trying to get through the wall of ITs.

But she just kept rocking.

"Ferris Boyd," RB sobbed. He was crawling toward her, like he would touch her.

"RB, stop," Delly commanded.

So he did.

"Come here," she said, and pulled him to her. Then they sat together, waiting for their friend.

After a long time, Ferris Boyd slowed down. After a long, long time, she stopped.

"Ferris Boyd," Delly asked, "can you hear me?"

The girl's right ear went up the tiniest bit.

Delly started in. "Danny Novello's an idiot."

Just the name made Ferris Boyd flinch.

Delly went on anyway. "You are not an IT. He's a chizzlehead."

The girl curled up even tighter.

"Shhh," RB's shush was so strong it sprayed her.

"What the...?" she yelled.

"You're hurting her more," he said.

And Delly saw it. She stopped.

RB scooched toward her, so he was at the edge of the ITs. "Ferris Boyd," he breathed, "you were amazing." His words were warm, fluffy clouds that floated over the ITs and surrounded her with softness.

"You got me free, and you saved Delly from fighting," he went on. "And you weren't mean. You were just good." RB's love clouds floated in her ears and drifted down to her heart.

"Ferris Boyd, you're my favorite," he said.

She raised her head to see him.

"You're not an IT," he whispered.

Her eyes winced with the word, but she stayed with him.

"You're the best person I know," he told her, leaning so their heads almost touched. "You're a hummin bin."

Ferris Boyd searched his eyes as if she was asking, Are you making fun of me, too?

Not looking away, he said, "Delly, tell about hummin bins."

"Why do you want—?"

"Just do it," he told her.

So she did. "A long time ago," she began, "Ma was helping me read. 'What's the title of the story?' she asked. 'Hummin Bins,' I read. The book was all about them.

"In the book, hummin bins made castles, and towers up to the sky. They tamed the animals, and took care of them. And hummin bins helped each other. They were always good.

"When I was done, Ma asked, 'Delly, what are hummin bins?' 'They're like people, but better,' I said. Then I told her, 'When I grow up, I'm going to live with the hummin bins,' and she smiled.

"But Galveston grabbed the book, 'Let me see that,' she said, and started laughing. 'This says human beings. There's no such thing as hummin bins.'

"'Ma, is that true?' I asked, and she nodded. "'How come you didn't tell me?' I cried.

"'I liked the hummin bins better, too,' she said."

When she was done, Delly gazed into the green for a while. Finally, she turned to her friend. "RB's right, Ferris Boyd. You are a hummin bin." Her eyeballs were wet, like they were swimming.

It was quiet, then, till RB's soft cloud voice said, "You're a hummin bin, too, Delly."

How could softness hurt? RB's words made her insides ache. She shook her head, remembering all the times she hadn't been.

"Right now you are," he told her.

She couldn't look at him, with her eyes pooling up, so she just pointed. "You are," she whispered, and sent a giant cloud of love at him.

And RB smiled, like she'd smothered him with fluff.

"Ferris Boyd," Delly asked, "can I please have your pen?"

Slowly, she passed it to her.

"Let's get rid of this chizzle," Delly said. She took the pen and turned every 'IT' into an 'H', then wrote 'ummin Bin' after it. When she was done, Ferris Boyd was surrounded by Hummin Bins. She was the biggest one of all.

The cat crawled into Ferris Boyd's lap as she read the words over and over.

Then there were no ITs at the hideawaysis; only hummin bins. "All right, then," Delly rasped, and they sat in the sweet softness of that.

At the whistle, the Pattisons headed home. It

wasn't till they were on the bridge that Delly asked RB, "So, Ferris Boyd's your favorite?" She didn't mind, mostly.

RB answered so fast, though, she knew he wasn't fibbing. "She's my favorite friend," he told her. "You're my favorite everything."

Then Delly's heart was up in her throat and she couldn't speak. So she nodded, because it was true for her, too.

Chapter 58

On Monday, Ferris Boyd was playing ball again. At the hideawaysis, there was no more rocking; she was reading her book.

"She's okay?" RB asked, and Delly nodded.

But sometimes she would catch the girl gazing out toward Brud Kinney's. She was missing him, and Delly knew it.

So Friday after supper, she snuck to Clarice.

"Ma," she whispered so RB couldn't hear her, "can I go ride my bike?"

"Why?" Clarice wanted to know.

"I want to practice with the big one," she told her, which was kind of true.

"Where?" Clarice went on.

"Out the River Road. There's no traffic. An hour." Delly answered all the questions her mom hadn't asked yet.

And Clarice nodded.

Delly'd had a bike, but it was tiny like a tricycle. So they gave her Galveston's old bike, but it was too big. She had to stand on steps to get on it. "Like a bawlgram horse," she rasped.

She rode it up on the highway, so she wouldn't go by the old Hennepin place, then down the dirt road to Kinney's. When she got there, Brud was playing ball in the drive.

Delly slowed the bike. "Bombs away!" she shouted, and flung herself off it, far away so it wouldn't fall on her. She watched it crash to the ground, then walked over to him. "Hey Brud Kinney," she said.

He stood there, stunned by the way she stopped a bike. Still, he raised one hand in a wave.

"What's up?" she asked.

Brud shrugged.

Then they both stood there. A lot like being

with Ferris Boyd, Delly thought.

Brud didn't know what to do, so he offered her the ball.

"Nah," she told him, "I hate that game." She sat on the stoop. "You go ahead, though."

So he did.

"Hot summer, huh?" Delly started out easy.

He nodded as he dribbled.

"Hey, Brud, I ever tell you my Ferris Boyd story?"

He winced, then shook his head.

"FerriDelly Tale Number One," she began. "The first time I see my...our friend Ferris Boyd."

Brud was facing the basket, so Delly didn't notice him turn red.

"I was at the IGA, waiting for my surpresent," she told him. "Finally, there it is, coming at me in the saddest-sounding car you ever heard. It pulls up right beside me, and you know what it is?"

Brud shrugged and shot the ball.

"A boy. A pale, skinny one, hunched over in his seat.

"Now that's no surpresent, Brud Kinney," Delly croaked. "It's chizzle."

"Next day I go to school, and there's that boy again. Lionel Terwilliger introduces him, 'This is Ms. Ferris Boyd.'"

Brud stopped, but Delly kept going.

"So I holler, 'That's no girl, that's a boy!' And Lionel Terwilliger yells at me, 'Ms. Pattison, this is Ms. Boyd,' like I'm an idierk.

"But, Brud, how was I supposed to know? She's got that short hair, she's wearing boys' clothes."

They were looking at each other now, Delly talking and Brud taking it in.

"He tells me the rest: She doesn't speak. Don't touch her. I'm thinking, Does she have two heads and a tail, too?"

Then there was no more story, just the truth. "Novello's right in a way, you know. She is an IT."

Brud's mouth dropped open, because Delly had said what he'd been thinking, what he felt so bad about.

"She's different. But it's not bad different; it's better.

"Because here's the thing," Delly told him, "I never had such a good time with anybody, and she doesn't even talk. Know what I mean?"

Brud nodded, because he did.

"She never hurts me. She just helps." The rasp was breaking up. "That's how she's an IT."

Brud turned away. "I th-th-thought he...sh-sh-she..."

"Me too," Delly said. "Still Ferris Boyd."

He remembered Sunday. "I m-m-messed up."

"I mess up more than anybody," she boasted. "She's still my friend."

He stared into the trees.

Just like Ferris Boyd, Delly thought. She looked at her watch. "Shikes, I got to go."

She brought the bike over to the steps. "Hey, will you hold this while I get on?"

So he did.

Then she was peddling hard down the drive. On the highway, she could hear RB, even though she was alone. "You're a hummin bin."

"Huh." She hoped that was true, and headed home.

Chapter 59

Sunday morning, Brud sat on his stoop staring at the street. Go, his heart told him. So he headed out on his bike.

But then he remembered how Ferris Boyd had looked at him while Novello called her an IT, and how he told her it was true. He pedaled back to his house.

Three times he started out; three times he came back. It was almost noon when his head had enough. Just do it, it commanded.

So he rode, slowly, out the River Road.

He stopped before the drive. He could see the top of her above the bushes, playing like nothing nobody'd ever seen, only better.

March, his head ordered, and sent him to the end of the drive.

Then Brud spotted the Pattisons. They'd been too tiny to see above the bushes. RB was playing ball, and Delly was sitting with that cat.

Brud's legs turned, taking him back to his bike.

Till Delly sighted him. "Hey, Brud Kinney!" she yelled.

RB and Ferris Boyd quit playing. "Hey, Brud," RB said, smiling.

And he couldn't escape.

"Come on over," RB hollered at him.

Brud glanced at Ferris Boyd.

She winced, as if seeing him hurt her. She looked at Delly.

"Come on, Brud Kinney," she told him.

Slowly, he shuffled up the drive. Then he stood there.

"Hey, Brud," Delly called to him, "I heard you quit playing ball with Novello."

Ferris Boyd's eyes came back to him.

Brud shrugged, because it was hard being proud of one thing when he'd messed up so many.

"I heard you told him to take back what he said," she went on, "but he wouldn't, so you quit."

Brud nodded once.

Then it was quiet, except for the birds. Brud didn't know what to do.

Delly decided it. "Ferris Boyd, we're going." She got up from the stoop.

"But I want to—," RB complained.

"RB, will you please come with me?" Delly asked, but it wasn't really a question, with her dragging him down the drive.

And they were gone.

Brud's foot scraped the concrete. It's time, his heart told him.

He didn't trust his mouth to do it. So he got his pad out of his pocket. He held it up to her. *Sorry*, it read, like he would say it: Not loud or quiet, just true.

She read it, and looked into his eyes. The word was there, too.

Brud tore out the page. He offered it to her.

Slowly, she took it. She folded it twice, and put it in her pocket.

You're done; you can go, his head said. Brud started to leave.

Till he heard a smack, smack, smack. Ferris Boyd was slapping her thigh, telling him, Stop.

So he did.

She took out her pad and pen, and scratched something. She passed it to him. A-N-T, it read, NO TOUCH.

It wasn't T-Y-R-R-A-N-A-S-A-U-R-U-S R-E-X. It wasn't even H-O-R-S-E. It was a new start.

Brud's smile was still sorry. Only the tips of his teeth glowed.

And she buried him. She beat him so bad he might as well have been a beginner.

It didn't matter. Boy or girl, losing by a little or a lot, playing with Ferris Boyd was still the best time he ever had.

After she skunked him, she went and stood by the door.

He put up his hand. See you next Sunday? it was asking.

It took a while for her to answer. Finally, she raised her hand. He heard it like a word: Yes.

Chapter 60

By the middle of August, it had been so long since trouble Delly hardly remembered the word. She'd had another Delly Day with Clarice. And now that Brud Kinney was back on Sundays, Ferris Boyd was better.

It was still the best summer ever. "There's just one thing I need to make it perfect," Delly decided.

Going over the bridge to the old Hennepin place, she checked the river. "It's time," she whispered.

She didn't say anything till just before the whistle. Then she announced, "Ferris Boyd, we're coming out at ten tomorrow. Be ready to go." The pinch of the paper reminded her. "Okay?"

"What are we doing?" RB asked.

"You'll see," she told him.

But he'd known her long enough. "A Dellyventure," he guessed. Then he started singing it, "We're going on a Dellyventure..."

Ferris Boyd looked scared.

"It'll be good," Delly assured her.

That didn't help.

It was RB singing, "Oh, Ferris Boyd, you got to go. We'll have a Dellyventure, tomor-r-ow," that calmed her.

That night, Delly crept around the house, scrounging up towels, a rope, and extra food. She got a swimsuit and boots from Gal's old clothes in the attic. She put matches in a plastic bag.

RB followed her, rubbing his hands together with happiness.

"Get your trunks and rain boots," she told him.

He took off. Two minutes later, he was back, singing, "Tomorrow's Dellyventure Day."

"Shhhh," she hushed him.

So he hummed it.

Chapter 61

The next morning, they were doing chores just after dawn.

"Why are you working now?" Clarice wondered.

"We're getgorlying," Delly explained.

And Clarice, running late, didn't ask what that meant.

They hid their packs till it was time. They were wearing the boots. Delly had Galveston's old ones strung around her neck, and the rope wrapped around her waist. At quarter to ten, they were tiptoeing to the door.

Till Galveston caught them. "Where are you two going so early?" she shouted.

"Is it early?" Delly asked innocently.

"It's not ten yet."

"Huh," she said.

Galveston gazed at Delly in her boot necklace and rope belt. "So strange," she sniffed. She shook her head at the two of them, wearing rainboots on a sunny day. "Go," she scowled.

So they did.

They sprinted all the way to Ferris Boyd's.

She was waiting on the stoop with the cat.

They stopped in front of her, grinning and gasping for air. Then RB started singing, "We're going on a Dellyventure," like they were headed to the North Pole to see Santa.

"Let's go," Delly declared.

But Ferris Boyd stayed, holding tight to the step.

Delly didn't blame her: The last time she'd taken her on a field trip, hard things had happened.

So she sat beside her. "Ferris Boyd," she asked, "you know how you got your hideawaysis, and you like it a lot?"

The girl turned to her.

"Well, I got one, too. I want to go to it. And I want you to go with me." She took a deep breath, because it was still hard asking the ones that mattered so much. "Will you please come with me?"

Ferris Boyd stared at the trees for a minute. Then she nodded.

"All right then." Delly grinned. "These boots are for you." She took them off her neck.

"We already got ours on," RB lifted one foot, then the other.

Ferris Boyd started untying her shoes, until Delly asked, "Hey, can you swim?"

Her fingers froze and her eyes shut tight. She whipped her head back and forth, No, No, No.

But Delly didn't talk loud or get worked up. "Ferris Boyd," she rasped softly, "You don't have to swim. You won't even get wet if you don't want to."

And the softness floated past the fear, so Ferris Boyd heard her. She opened her eyes.

"I promise," Delly told her.

Still, she took a long time putting on those boots.

All the while, the cat's tail was flicking against the concrete, like it had something to say. "Maoh," it called.

"What?" Delly answered.

With a growl it warned her, She'd better be all right.

Delly leaned close to it. "Promise," she said.

The cat lay down on the stoop, as if it would wait there till Ferris Boyd came back.

Delly turned to the other two. "Let's go."

"To Delly's hideawaysis," RB sang.

Then the three chumbudions went down the road to the river.

Chapter 62

Most days, the river that ran through town was wide as Main Street. But August had been dry. It had starved the river skinny, so the sides were just rocks and sand.

"See, Ferris Boyd." Delly pointed. "It's like a path."

The girl nodded.

"I'll go first," Delly told them. "Then Ferris Boyd." She took the rope from her waist. "We'll tie ourselves to each other."

Ferris Boyd's eyes opened wide.

"It's for RB," Delly whispered, "so he doesn't get separated," which was almost the truth.

They strung the rope through their belt loops. They hiked along the bank. The birds sang with RB, "We're going to Delly's hideawaysis."

After a while, though, RB quit singing and started asking questions. "Is it on the river?" he wondered.

"Sort of," she told him.

"How'd you find it?"

"In Clayton Fitch's canoe."

"When are we going to get there?"

Delly didn't know, though; she'd traveled a lot faster in a boat. "Soon," she said.

But RB wouldn't let it go, asking every two minutes, "Are we there yet?"

The question was like sandpaper on her skin; it was rubbing her raw. "RB," she yelled, "how about you slap that question on some bread and swallow it?"

Then he was quiet. For about a second.

"Delly, I'm hot," he whined.

"Yep."

"I'm thirsty."

"Yep."

" I'm—"

We're there!" she shouted.

They'd come around a bend. The rest of the river went straight ahead. But a branch broke off from it, cutting in front of them. It disappeared into the trees.

They followed it. It flowed into the woods, then turned back to the river, making an island on the far side of it. On this side, though, was a beach. In front of the beach, the water got deep and wide. It was a pool.

"Oh, Delly." RB sighed.

She pointed up the hill behind the beach. There was a big rock with a flat top covered with moss, like a tablecloth.

"Can we eat there?" he asked.

Delly nodded, then she turned to her friend. "Ferris Boyd, this is our other hideawaysis." She spread her arms wide, as if she would give it all to her.

Ferris Boyd put her hands over of her mouth,

like she had to hold the happiness in.

"Come on," Delly told them, and they toured the place. They went to the stone table and rubbed the moss. They peered into the pool. They sat side by side on the beach.

"It's like somebody made it just for us." RB said it, but they all nodded.

"Delly?" he asked.

"Huh."

"Can we go swimming?"

"Yep," she answered.

She opened her pack. "Ferris Boyd," she said, slow and easy, "you don't have to go in the water, but I brought these for you." She set the suit and towel next to her. "If you want to swim, I'll teach you."

Then she asked, "Do you want to go swimming with us?"

She didn't do it right away, but the girl shook her head, No.

"Okay," Delly said softly, and she and RB went to the woods to change.

Two minutes later, they came tearing down the beach. "Whoohoohoo," RB screamed. "Happy Hallelujah!" Delly hollered, as they hurled themselves at the water.

They played Shark and Scared Swimmer. They played Tidal Wave. They raced back and forth across the pool. All the while, Ferris Boyd watched.

Delly stopped. "Ferris Boyd," she called, "the water's only up to my neck. It'd be up to your belly. Want to come in?"

She took longer to do it; still, her head said, No.

The Pattisons played Divers of the Deep. They held their breaths for as long as they could underwater.

So they didn't see her disappear. Next thing they knew, she was standing at the edge of the pool, wearing Gal's suit with her t-shirt over it.

"Hey," RB greeted her. "Want to come in?"

She stared at the water as if it might bite her. She took tiny steps till she was in it to her hips.

"Ferris Boyd," Delly asked, "want me to teach you?"

It was the smallest nod, like a whispered, "Maybe."

"I want to teach, too," RB piped up.

"You be the demonstrator," Delly told him.

"I'm the demonstrator," he sang.

"First, you got to hold your breath and put your head in the water," Delly taught her. "You have to blow air out your nose, so the water doesn't go up it."

RB nodded. "That hurts."

"Show her," Delly said.

He took a big breath and went under. Bubbles floated around his head. He was grinning when he popped up again. "That's how you do it."

"Okay, Ferris Boyd, now you," Delly directed.

Slowly, she submerged herself. She wasn't under for two seconds till she shot out of the water, sputtering.

"You're all right," Delly said gently, and that calmed her.

RB showed her how to kick, and how to scoop water with her hands. Then he put the whole thing together. "Just like Tuba." He laughed as he paddled around the pool.

"Now you try," Delly told her. "Stand up when you want to stop."

They watched her push off. They watched her arms and legs splash. They watched her sink to the bottom of the pool.

"That's it," Delly cheered when she came up. "You just got to go faster."

She tried again. This time, her arms and legs were outboard motors. She cruised across the water.

"You're swimming, Ferris Boyd, you're swimming!" RB clapped.

Then there was no stopping her; she kept going around and around the pool.

Finally, Ferris Boyd ran out of gas. She stood in the pool, panting.

Delly was deciding what to teach her next. "Dead man's float or frog kick?"

"No more lessons," RB announced. "Let's eat."

They went to the stone table. Delly laid everything on the moss like a holiDelly feast.

"Puhlease pawss the peanut buttah and jelly sawndwiches." RB said.

"What's the matter with your mouth?" Delly asked.

"We're eating on a tablecloth," he whispered. "I'm having manners."

"Then stawp tawking with your mouwuth full," she told him, and that ended it. For about a second.

"Ferris Boyud, would you like some watuh?" he inquired. He wiped the lip of the bottle with his towel before handing it to her.

When they were done, RB and Ferris Boyd started cleaning up.

"Hold on," Delly said. "Dessert."

She went in her pack and pulled out a bag of the big marshmallows, and a jar of fudge sauce. "For dipping," she told them.

"Ooooh," RB sighed.

Ferris Boyd's eyes got wide.

They sunk the marshmallows into the fudge,

like they were drowning. "I'll save you," RB would shout, and pull them out. Then they popped them in their mouths.

When they were done, RB looked like he'd been dipped in fudge, too. "Deeelishaws," he declared.

Chapter 63

After lunch, they lay down on the sand with their bellies up, like beached whales.

RB and Ferris Boyd closed their eyes. Delly stayed till their breaths were sleeping ones, then went to work.

When she was done, she touched RB's shoulder. "Ferris Boyd," she whispered, "time to get up."

RB was rubbing his eyes. "Did you sleep?"

She shook her head. "I got wood for next time, for a fire." She pointed to the pile. "I buried the matches by it, so we don't have to bring them."

Ferris Boyd watched her.

"What are you going to name it?" RB wondered.

"What?"

"Your hideawaysis."

She thought about it: Dellyland, The Delaware Territory. "Delaferbia," she finally said. She wrote it in the sand so they could see it.

"Hey, that's part of our names," he exclaimed.

Ferris Boyd traced the word with her finger, as if she was saying it to herself.

RB grabbed a stick. He marched around the beach waving it over his head, like a flag. In a deep voice he hollered, "I hereby name this place Delaferbia," and planted it in the sand.

Then he asked, "Del?"

"Huh."

"Can we go in again?"

Delly glanced at Ferris Boyd. She wanted it, too.

"For a little while," she told them.

Those two ran into the water. But Delly had to wait till her heart quit pounding so hard with happiness, because they loved the place like she did.

"Let's be dolphins," RB shouted.

Ferris Boyd was nodding.

"Okay," she agreed.

"I'll show you how." RB squatted down at the bottom of the pool, then pushed off so he flew into the air. He wiggled like a fish till he flopped in the water.

"Now you do it," he said.

So they did.

And it was fun, shooting into the air like sea-to-sky missiles. When Ferris Boyd hit the water, her shirt floated up around her armpits like a jellyfish.

Delly was crouched at the bottom of the pool, about to blast off. Ferris Boyd came down with her back to Delly and her shirt up.

And Delly saw it.

In the water, they were purple. They were slashes across her skin, like a message written in code. A bad message, ripped into Ferris Boyd's back.

It was ugly. It was awful. Delly didn't want to know it.

Ferris Boyd shot into the air again.

But Delly could still see the message. She could

almost feel it, the pain that would etch flesh.

She retched. Water went up her nose and down her windpipe. She came up gagging.

The other two stopped when they heard her hacking. "You okay?" RB asked.

Delly wouldn't look at Ferris Boyd. She didn't want to see the message in her eyes, in the way her body hunched over.

"Time to go," she told them.

They went to the woods to change. They met back at the beach, with Ferris Boyd wearing her wet shirt.

RB gazed at the woods, the beach, the water. "Nobody would ever find us here," he breathed, and Ferris Boyd nodded. "Good-bye, Delaferbia." He waved to it.

Ferris Boyd picked up some sand, and put it in her pocket, as if she would take the day with her.

"Let's go," Delly ordered.

So they tied themselves together, and headed back to River Bluffs.

Chapter 64

All the way home, the message wouldn't leave Delly alone. She was almost glad for RB's questions.

"Can we come back tomorrow?" he asked.

"Gal'll get suspicious."

"Next week?"

"I don't know."

"Every week?"

"RB!" she shouted. She never wanted to come back. She'd forget the day if she could.

"Delly?"

"What?"

"This was the best day ever."

"Huh," she answered. Because it was. Then it

was the worst.

But if the message was true, every day was the worst for Ferris Boyd.

At the bridge, they untied themselves. Ferris Boyd walked beside Delly out the River Road. RB ran up ahead, singing, "We're from Delaferbia."

The question had been there before they were dolphins. It had been there since the day the green Impala was in the drive. Delly didn't want to ask it.

It came out of her, anyway. Soft and sad, it whispered, "Ferris Boyd, what does that man do to you?"

Ferris Boyd flinched, as if something had hit her. She stopped. Slowly, she turned to Delly.

Delly stopped, but she stared at the road. She was too scared to see what the girl would do. Would she run? Would she tell her about the ugly awfulness? Which would be worse?

RB heard the silence behind him, and spun around. "Hey," he said, smiling. Then he saw their faces. "Hey?"

Ferris Boyd turned back to the road. She started shuffling again.

And Delly followed. For once, she was glad not to get an answer.

When they got to the old Hennepin place, the cat ran to them. It bumped their shins with its back.

Ferris Boyd took off the boots. She held them out to Delly.

"You keep them," RB told her, "for next time."

But she kept pushing them toward Delly. She could forget the day, and what she'd seen, if she wanted.

Delly could feel the friend paper in her pocket. It was pressing her, Look at Ferris Boyd.

So she did. She glanced at the girl's face. And it wasn't ugly, or awful, like the message. It was just her friend.

Then Delly wouldn't forget the day, or even seeing the message. It was all Ferris Boyd; it was all her friend. "Keep them, for next time," she told her.

Slowly, Ferris Boyd pulled them to herself.

The whistle blew.

"See you tomorrow, Ferris Boyd," RB sang.

"See you tomorrow," Delly promised.

At the bridge, RB asked her, "Del, what's wrong?"

Delly wouldn't tell him, though. There was nothing he could do, and he'd stop singing if he knew.

So she took his hand, and he let her hold it all the way home.

That night, Delly went to Clarice. She didn't ask; she just crawled in beside her.

"Ma," she rasped.

Clarice kept snoring.

Delly didn't mind. She needed to talk; she wasn't sure she wanted Clarice hearing her. "It's Ferris Boyd. She's..." and the rasp cracked apart. Her body shook with sobs that couldn't come out.

"Hunnhhh?" Clarice stirred.

Delly held herself still till Clarice was sleeping again. Then she said, loud enough for her mom to almost hear it, "It's bad, Ma. But I can't tell you because..." She didn't know what would happen, but she was sure it'd be terrible. "Ma, I don't know what to do."

Clarice snored once, then rolled onto her side. She threw her arm over Delly, and pulled her tight.

And Clarice was a love shield, her warm softness all around Delly so nothing bad could get to her.

In the warm softness of Clarice, Delly got drowsy. But she couldn't quit thinking about Ferris Boyd, hurting all alone, with nobody like Clarice to hold her.

"I'll take care of you," she told the darkness.

And she did.

She brought extra sandwiches to the hideawaysis. She went to the library, and got books on animals for her friend.

"This one's about the creatures of Alaska," she told her. "And this one's just about cats."

"What kind of cat is Mowr?" RB wondered.

"A bawlgram cat," she answered, and it flicked its tail at her.

She didn't ask Ferris Boyd any more questions. And when RB wanted to go back to Delaferbia, she told him, "The river's too high, from the rain," which was close-to-honest.

Every day put time and happiness between them and the message, so Delly could almost believe it wasn't true.

Chapter 65

It was September. It was school again.

The night before it started, Delly announced, "Ma, I'm thinking I'll do another project this year. After school." Then she asked, "Okay?"

"And I'm still helping," RB added.

"What happened to the other one?" Clarice wondered.

"Oh, that's over," Delly said, like it was old news.

"And what's this one going to be about?"

"Human beings," she answered.

"Hummin bins." RB whispered, and Delly pinched him.

Clarice quit fixing food and stared at her daughter. She could barely remember the last time Verena's siren had screamed down the street, or she'd had to pry Delly's fingers off Galveston's body. Now here Delly was, before school even started, thinking about extra work she wanted to do. Clarice was so happy, it leaked out her eyeballs.

Delly got nervous. "Ma?" she rasped.

"Okay." Clarice smiled.

The first day of sixth grade was like a surpresent: Ferris Boyd was in Delly's class again; Novello wasn't. And Lionel Terwilliger had moved up a grade to teach them.

"Happy Hallelujah," Delly exclaimed when she saw him.

"I appreciate your expression of pleasure, Ms. Pattison," he replied.

At three o'clock, the three chumbudions met at the back door. The sun was shining as they strolled across the playground. RB was singing, "It's school again but that's okay. We're going to the hideawaysis today," and Delly was humming along.

Till she spotted him. She hadn't seen him since that day in the park, but the fury hadn't forgotten.

He was walking with his back to her. He was wearing a red shirt, like a target. A nasty, name-calling, needing-to-be-taken-down target.

She stopped in the grass. She turned her fists into balls of fight. Like a human cannon, she fired herself.

"Chizzlehead!" she shouted as she flew at him.

He turned, and she landed on his chest. He fell backwards, screaming, "Ayeeeee!"

He hit the ground hard. "Oooooof," he groaned as the wind went out of him, and she pinned him.

That quick, there was a crowd of kids around them. "Fight! Fight!" they yelled.

"Stop," RB hollered, but his voice was too tiny to get through.

As soon as he got some air, Novello started gasping, "You...My...Smelly," the meanness and the love fighting for his mouth.

Delly hacked up a giant goober. She set it on her

bottom lip, so he'd know what was coming. Then she puckered up, to give him the biggest wet one ever.

"Nooooo," he howled.

There was a voice, a deeper one, in the distance. "What's going on over there?" Ms. Niederbaum bellowed.

But Delly couldn't hear her for the screams.

Ferris Boyd was standing in the grass. She watched Delly take the Nasty One down. She saw Ms. Niederbaum barreling over, yelling "Break it up!" In a minute, Delly would be on her way to another school.

There was one more voice, then. It was not pale and skinny; it was loud and strong. It blasted through the crowd. "Delly," it cried, "run!"

Delly'd never heard the voice before, but she knew it. "Later," she smirked, and jumped off Novello. She scooted through legs and got free of the crowd.

Ferris Boyd and RB were at the edge of it.

"Let's go," she rasped, and they ran, across the playground, over the bridge, and out the River Road.

When Ms. Niederbaum got to the crowd, it went quiet. She stood over Novello. "Who did this to you?" she demanded.

His mouth pinched and puckered as love and meanness fought for his soul. Finally, he muttered, "Nobody."

Love had won.

They went straight to the hideawaysis. Delly was on her back, rolling and laughing like a pig in a pool of mud. "That was perfect. Did you see him go down? Did you see his face?"

"Delly," RB called, but she didn't hear him.

"One more second," she crowed, "and he would have been covered in spit. If it wasn't for that Ms. Niederbaum…"

"But you saved me, Ferris Boyd," she went on. "You hollered and I heard you."

Suddenly, she was still. "Ferris Boyd, I heard you," she breathed. She turned to her friend. "I heard you!"

Ferris Boyd was not laughing. She was rocking

back and forth, fast. Her eyes were wild, and her hands were clamped over her mouth.

"Ferris Boyd?" Delly crawled to her. "Hey, Ferris Boyd."

The girl only went faster.

"Delly, stop," RB told her

"But she spoke. She saved me. That's not bad; that's good. Isn't it?"

"She's really scared," he answered.

Delly could see it. So she sat beside RB, and they waited for their friend.

After a long time, Ferris Boyd slowed down. After a long, long time, she stopped. Still, she muzzled her mouth.

Slowly, Delly inched toward her. "Ferris Boyd, listen." She used RB's soft cloud voice to say it. "Nobody heard you except me and RB. And we won't tell anybody. Promise."

The girl's eyes searched Delly's, asking, Are you sure?

"Sure," she replied.

Little by little, her body uncurled, but her hands

kept clutching her mouth.

RB took her book from her bag, and snuggled in beside her. He turned the page from time to time, but Ferris Boyd just stared into the green.

Delly sat across from them, her brain bursting with questions. Can you talk all the time? How did I know it was you? How could saving somebody be wrong? they wanted to know.

But she saw the fear in her friend's eyes, and stayed still.

The whistle blew.

Delly let RB go first. At the ladder she rasped, "Ferris Boyd?"

Her friend turned to her.

"You're the best surpresent ever," she whispered.

Ferris Boyd closed her eyes, as if she was taking the words to a place deep inside her.

When she opened them again, they were asking, Will it be all right? They were hoping and needing and praying.

So Delly nodded, hoping and needing and praying, too.

Chapter 66

It was amazing, how many kids heard Ferris Boyd holler, "Delly, run!" "Ferris Boyd can talk," they told each other.

By the next morning, the speech therapist, the school counselor, and the principal knew it, too.

They called her to the office. They had lots of questions, like, "What happened yesterday?" "Why did you speak?" and "Can you do it again?"

The girl was silent.

They brought the green Impala to school. It was in the parking lot for an hour. Through Math and Social Studies, Ferris Boyd watched it out the window.

At the end of the day, she moved so slowly she was almost walking backwards.

"What's wrong?" RB asked.

"The green Impala was here," Delly answered.

"Oh," he sighed. He turned to Ferris Boyd. He raised his hand, and wrapped his tiny fingers around hers.

Her fingers curled around his, and held tight.

RB grabbed Delly with his other hand. "We're the three chumbudions," he tried to sing, but his voice was cracking.

They trudged out the River Road. When they got near the old Hennepin place, they saw it in the drive. They stopped.

"Ferris Boyd," Delly whispered, as if the car could hear, "you want us to come with you?"

She shook her head.

"You want to come home with us?"

"Yes," RB exclaimed. "You could stay with us."

Ferris Boyd stared at the green Impala, as if she was asking it, Would you know where I go? Could you find me? She shook her head again.

Delly leaned close to her friend. "I'm so sorry," she rasped.

The girl's eyes gazed deep into Delly's. There was no blame, only the bluest sadness.

Then she shuffled to the house, and went inside.

The Pattisons headed for the ditch. The cat met them there.

Right away, the pale skinny ghost was in the window. It put its hand against the glass. Go, it told them. Or, Good-bye. Then it was gone.

They stayed till the whistle, but they didn't see her again.

That night, Delly didn't go to Clarice, because RB came to her. He crawled in bed and curled up beside her, and she couldn't leave him.

"Maybe he'll go away again," he whispered.

"Huh," Delly answered, because she wouldn't take that hope from him.

After a while, he asked "Del, should we tell Ma?"

"Tell her what?" she asked back. "About us being out there every day with nobody watching us?"

"About him." RB was sobbing.

So she said softly, "What about him, RB?"

"That he...that he..." But there was no finishing it, because he didn't know. Only Ferris Boyd did, and she wasn't telling.

Delly put her arm over him, and they pretended to sleep.

Chapter 67

During the night, Delly put together a plan: In the morning, she and RB would run out to the old Hennepin place, and walk Ferris Boyd to school.

She woke him early. They were racing around the house, trying to get ready.

"Hurry up," she told him.

"I know," he told her back.

"Hey, Ma, we got to go," she hollered. "Okay?"

They didn't wait for an answer. They shot out the back door.

And almost fell over the packages on the porch.

Delly's name was on the box; RB's was on the bag. "Surpresents!" he exclaimed.

RB opened his first. "Ferris Boyd's book," he breathed, and hugged it to him.

Delly reached for the box.

"Maoh," it cried.

She jumped back. "What the glub?" she rasped.

"Maooooh," it yowled, from inside.

"Mowr." RB smiled, and lifted it out. He cuddled it, and the cat purred.

"Won't she miss Mowr?" he wondered.

Delly didn't answer; she was thinking. "RB," she finally said, "take the book and go to school. I got to take care of that cat."

"What about meeting Ferris Boyd?"

"She was already here," Delly explained. "She left her house a long time ago."

"She's at school?" he asked.

"Huh," she answered, because she hoped so.

"I want to stay with you," he insisted.

"RB, I need you to do this for me. Please?" She wasn't asking; she was begging.

"Okay," he agreed, and took off.

She snuck the cat to her room. She put it in her

closet with food and water and a bunch of paper in the box. "You got to go in there," she told it. "And be quiet. You hear me?"

"Maoh," it whispered.

Then she ran, through backyards and over fences, the fastest way to school.

She checked the classroom first; it was empty.

She went to the back door. The first bell rang, but there was no Ferris Boyd.

The second bell rang. The corridors cleared, except for Delly.

And Ms. Niederbaum. She was rounding up latecomers and lolligaggers. She grabbed her by the shoulder.

"Ferris Boyd's not here," Delly rasped.

"But you are," Ms. Niederbaum replied, and escorted her to her room.

"Ferris Boyd isn't here," she told Lionel Terwilliger.

"That is true, Ms. Pattison," he answered. "Please be seated."

But she couldn't.

"I'm not feeling good," she said. "Can I please go?" She pointed toward the nurse's office, next to the exit.

She did look ill. Lionel Terwilliger nodded.

Delly stood by the door for a moment. It could be big trouble; maybe being sent away trouble. But the friend paper in her pocket was pressing.

"For Ferris Boyd," she whispered. Then she ran, across the playground and out the River Road.

She slowed at the end of the drive, because the green Impala was there.

It couldn't stop her, though. She ran to the door and banged on it. "Ferris Boyd," she hollered. 'Ferris Boyd!"

The man opened it.

For a second, Delly couldn't speak. Because, up close, he looked like a dad, not somebody to be scared of. "F-F-Ferris Boyd?" she sputtered.

"She's at school," the man said. And he sounded like a dad, not somebody who made marks on a girl's back. "Who are you?"

"I'm her friend." Delly's voice got stronger saying that. "Petunia Poopenhagen."

"How come you're not in school?" He squinted at her.

"I'm...I'm...," Delly stammered, "I'm late!" She took off down the drive.

She pretended to head toward town, then dove in the ditch and backtracked to the woods. She climbed to the hideawaysis. "Ferris Boyd," she called, "it's me."

But there was no Ferris Boyd. No birds, either, as if they'd migrated overnight. Other things were missing, too: The extra food, the blanket, the boots.

Delly sat alone in the hideawaysis, and the questions came at her. Is he hiding her? Did he hurt her? Is she...? She couldn't finish the last one.

She started shaking. This was trouble. Not tiny getting grounded trouble. This was her friend gone missing, maybe worse, trouble. It was more trouble than Delly could handle. "What do I do?" she gasped.

There was only one person who could handle this much trouble. "Bawldoublegrammit," Delly grimaced. She was desperate, though.

"For Ferris Boyd," she told herself. Then she scrambled down the tree and sprinted into town.

Chapter 68

Ms. Niederbaum had seen a child, a tiny one with copper curls, tearing across the playground. She checked with Lionel Terwilliger, then she called the police.

Officer Tibbetts hung up the phone. She grabbed her keys and handcuffs. She was on her way to catch a tiny, copper-curled school-skipper.

And Delly burst into the station. "Ferris Boyd's gone," she declared.

Officer Tibbetts shook her head; she knew Delly's tricks. "To the cruiser," she ordered.

So she screamed it. "Ferris Boyd is disappeared!"

"Hey!" Verena shouted back, but she saw how

worked up the child was. "Tell me without yelling," she commanded.

Delly took a breath. "Ferris Boyd's not in school, so I went to her house. He says she went early—"

"Who's he?" Verena interrupted.

"The man in the green Impala. Her dad."

"Then you're both skipping school," the policewoman pronounced.

"Yes. No." Verena was messing her up. "Listen: Something's wrong. Bad wrong. I'm afraid...," Delly could only whisper it, "he hurt her."

"Why do you think that?" Officer Tibbetts inquired.

So Delly told about how Ferris Boyd didn't talk and you couldn't touch her. She told how the green Impala was almost never at the old Hennepin place, but when it was the girl sent them away. She described the marks on Ferris Boyd's back. Then she told about Ferris Boyd saying two words, and everything getting worse. "Now she's giving her stuff away, and the boots and the blanket are gone"

Officer Tibbetts listened. Then she asked, "Did she say her dad hurt her?"

"She doesn't talk!" Delly exploded. "Now you got to help me find her before...before..."

"Delly," the policewoman told her, "her father should be the one reporting her missing. I can check with him and the school—"

But Delly'd been in enough trouble to know the rules. "Ferris Boyd is truant. I'm reporting her. Now you got to go get her."

Verena studied her, searching for signs of monkey business. All she found was a scared kid. "All right," she decided. "Let's go."

When they got to the cruiser, Delly went to sit in back like the criminals. "Up front," the policewoman ordered.

Officer Tibbetts went into the school alone. When she was done asking her questions, she told them, "Delly Pattison's with me."

They drove to the old Hennepin place.

"You stay in the car," Verena told her.

So she did. She opened the window so she could hear.

"I'm Officer Tibbetts," the policewoman was saying. "I'd like to see Ferris Boyd."

"She's at school," the man replied.

"She's not at school," Officer Tibbetts informed him. "Do you know where she is?"

The man was quiet for a minute. "She'll show up."

"Any of her stuff missing?"

"It's packed," he said.

"For what?"

"We're moving."

"Hmm." Verena let that sit for a bit. Then she asked, "You got a number I can call if I find her?"

"I don't need you looking for Ferris," the man told her. "I'll find her myself."

Officer Tibbetts wouldn't be told. "You let me know if she shows up. And I will be looking for her."

As soon as Verena got back in the cruiser, Delly whispered, "Do you think he hurt her?"

"Not sure," she answered. "She might have run away."

"She left us?" Delly rasped.

"She didn't leave you," Officer Tibbetts explained. "She left him."

"But she could have come with us."

"Maybe she didn't want to get you in trouble. Or she didn't think anybody could help her."

"I would have helped her," she argued. "She's my friend."

Officer Tibbetts turned to Delly. "Sometimes, when someone's been hurt a lot, the perpetrator seems very powerful. Too powerful to stop. The victim thinks the best she can do is try to get away."

The policewoman started the car. "Now let's find your friend."

Delly's eyeballs were swimming. As they drove, she put her head out the window so the breeze would dry them.

When they passed over the bridge, she glanced at the river. It was down some since the rains. You could walk it, with boots.

Chapter 69

At the station, Officer Tibbetts sat Delly at her desk. "Write down everybody she knows and all the places she might go," she directed.

Me, Delly wrote first. RB, Brud Kinney, the cat, the birds, the old Hennepin place, the hideawaysis.

That was it. She was putting down the pen.

And Clayton Fitch stormed in the door, squawking, "Verena, Norma saw that bad Pattison running to the river this morning."

That's when the idea hit Delly, like a smack to the brain. "Jiminy fipes," she gasped, "I know…"

Then she stopped. She glanced at Officer Tibbetts, with her big voice and her gun, and she knew what Ferris Boyd would feel.

So while Clayton Fitch squealed, "You going to put her behind bars this time? Huh?" Delly snuck out of the station.

"I'm coming, Ferris Boyd," she rasped as she ran to the river.

She was so focused, she didn't hear the crunch, crunch of police boots behind her. Suddenly, something had her by the armpits. Next thing she knew, she was nose-to-nose with Verena again.

"Where are you going?" the policewoman asked.

"Where do you think I'm going?" Delly asked back.

"Do you know where she is?"

"How would I know where she is?"

"Delly!" Officer Tibbetts bellowed. "You need to tell me so I can protect her!"

Delly gazed into Verena's eyes, like Ferris Boyd would, to see if she was true. And she saw it: The policewoman wanted to help.

So she told her, sadly, "You can't come. You'll scare her. I got to go alone."

Officer Tibbetts softened. "Delly," she said, "what if she's sick or hurt and you can't help her? What if he finds her first?"

Delly hadn't considered that.

"Let's figure out a way we can go together, without scaring her," the policewoman offered.

Delly thought about it. "You can't touch her," she warned. "She'll go wild."

Verena nodded. "I'll only touch her if she's unsafe and I can't help her otherwise."

"You got to keep her safe from him," Delly demanded.

"If we find her," Verena said, "I will keep her safe."

"And you won't send her away. She'll be too scared."

"Delly, I can't..." Officer Tibbetts wavered.

"That's the deal," she insisted.

"Okay," the policewoman agreed.

Delly nodded. "She went down the river, to Delaferbia."

Officer Tibbetts set the girl on the ground.

"Let's go."

"Will you call my Ma?" Delly asked. "RB'll worry."

So she did. "She's not in trouble," Verena told Clarice. "She's helping me."

The police kept a boat by the river. Delly'd never borrowed that one because it had a motor, although she'd thought about it. They sat in the back, beside each other.

"A lot of birds on the river," Officer Tibbetts noticed.

Delly just sniffed.

Because when Delly Pattison finally cried, it didn't come bawling out of her. The tears poured silently, down her cheeks and onto her shirt. Two streams of snot followed. She stared ahead, wiping the snot with her sleeve and sniffing.

It was the sniffling that made Officer Tibbetts look. She passed Delly a handkerchief, and that got her sobbing.

"It's my fault," she cried. "She talked so I

wouldn't get in trouble."

"Delly," the policewoman said softly, "do you know why a person stops speaking?"

She shook her head.

"It's because she's been hurt her so badly, she doesn't have words for it. Or somebody's told her he'll hurt her if she talks. She thinks her voice can't help her.

"Ferris Boyd talking is a good thing. It means, for a moment, she thought her words could help."

"But now we don't know if she's run away or if she's..." Delly couldn't say it.

"Ferris Boyd's survived a lot," the policewoman told her. "She's stronger than you think."

That helped a little. Delly honked into the handkerchief.

"You need to know something." Officer Tibbetts stared hard at her. "The only person who's at fault is the person who hurt her."

"But I saw the marks, and I didn't tell." Delly wept.

The policewoman nodded. "You were scared."

That was only part of it, though. "I didn't want it to be true," she sobbed.

"Me neither," Verena sighed. "Nobody does. But it is."

And it was awful, knowing there was such badness in the world. It was good, though, hearing somebody tell the truth. Because the badness had been there all along. Now they could stop it.

Verena watched the river as she spoke. "Out of all the people who know Ferris Boyd, you're the only one who figured out what was going on. You're the only one who's here, trying to help her.

"Delly," she said, "you're a good kid."

Delly gazed at Officer Tibbetts. Any other day, she would have rather been buried in cow patties than sitting next to her. Now, there was nobody she'd rather be beside. "Verena?" she rasped.

The policewoman glanced over.

Delly's red, leaky eyes told her, "Thanks."

Verena nodded, and turned back to the river.

Chapter 70

When they got close to Delaferbia, Delly raised her hand and Officer Tibbetts killed the motor. They drifted into the bank.

"I go," Delly mouthed, and the policewoman nodded.

There were bootprints, Galveston-sized ones, all over the beach. Some of the wood was stacked for a fire.

Delly'd never been so happy. "You're alive!" she wanted to whoop. But she'd never been so sad, either, knowing her friend was all alone, thinking nobody could help her.

So instead she said, "Ferris Boyd, I'm here."

There was no reply.

"Ferris Boyd," Delly asked, "will you please come to me?"

She didn't.

Delly searched the place. She looked behind the stone table, up in the trees, down into the pool. She couldn't find her.

She sat on the beach. "What am I going to do?"

There was one more thing Delly could try. "Tell the truth," she grimaced. But it was for her friend.

"Okay Ferris Boyd," she rasped, "here's the truth: I know he hurts you. I didn't do anything because I was scared, but I was wrong."

Nothing made a sound except the birds, chirping over her words. She'd have to tell more truths.

"Okay, here's the real truth: I know you ran away. I know you think you got to do this on your own. But you're my best friend; I want to help."

Still, there were only birds.

"Shush, birds," she said.

Then she took a minute, because the last one was the hardest to tell.

"Okay Ferris Boyd, here's the real, real truth: You know all those creatures you take care of? Well, I'm the wildest one of all. I wouldn't be okay without you." The rasp cracked. "Please don't leave me."

All those years of not crying, and Delly was doing it twice in one day.

The birds were cawing now, like they were calling her, "Crybaby."

Delly looked over at them to yell, "Quit it, you bawlgram birds!" And she saw it.

There was a hole in the hill, like a cave. It had brush in front of it, so she hadn't spotted it before. Those birds were all around it.

"Holy shikes," she exclaimed, and ran to it. She pushed the brush aside.

Ferris Boyd was curled up inside, wrapped in the blanket and wearing Galveston's boots. Happy Hallelujah! Delly wanted to holler.

Till she saw her friend's eyes. They weren't happy; they were terrified.

So Delly sat just outside the cave. She didn't stir, or say a word.

After a while, she turned so her friend could see her eyes. "Ferris Boyd, do you know I wouldn't hurt you?" she asked softly.

The girl nodded.

"I want to keep you safe, but I can't do it on my own. So I brought somebody to help us."

Ferris Boyd's body stiffened.

"It's Officer Tibbetts," Delly told her. "She promised she'll protect you. She promised she won't send you away."

Just like that, Ferris Boyd's arms flipped up in front of her. Her legs kicked off the blanket. She was going to bolt.

And Delly was crying again. "Ferris Boyd, if you want to run, I'll keep them busy. I'll do whatever you want. But what if you get sick? What if he finds you?

"I don't want you to be all alone." she sobbed. "I don't want you to get hurt anymore. But we need help." She moved aside, and waited for her friend to fly past her.

Then she waited some more.

Ferris Boyd stayed in the cave, though. After a long time, her arms settled at her sides. After a long, long time, her eyes stopped screaming and came back to Delly.

They were full of questions. There were so many they tumbled over each other: Where will I stay? What will she do to me? How can she stop him?

Delly told the truth. "I don't know. But she promised, and I believe her."

Ferris Boyd got her pad and pen. She wrote something, and passed it to Delly. DAD, it read, in small, shaky letters. After everything, she was worried for him, too.

Delly thought about how, for all her trouble, Boomer had never hurt her. She thought about what somebody would have to do to make a girl not talk, not want to be touched.

She took the paper. She ripped it into tiny pieces. "That's no dad," she said.

Ferris Boyd stared into the trees for a long time. Then she crawled out of the cave, and stood. She wasn't leaving; she was waiting.

Delly stood beside her. "All right then," she rasped. She led her down the beach to the boat.

Officer Tibbetts was waiting.

Ferris Boyd took one look at the policewoman and the boat, and her body started shaking.

Delly saw it. "You got a rope in there?" she asked.

Verena rummaged around and threw it to her.

Delly handed one end to her friend, and they tied themselves to each other.

"You want to go first?" Delly let her decide.

Ferris Boyd shook her head.

"We're walking," she told the policewoman.

And that's how they got back to River Bluffs: The two friends trudging along the river, and the boat with Officer Tibbetts following behind.

Chapter 71

As the three of them hiked up the bank from the boat dock, they spotted it: The green Impala was parked in front of the police station.

And the next thing she knew, Delly was on her rear end, bouncing down the bank.

Ferris Boyd was walking fast, but backwards. She was dragging Delly with her.

"Hey, Verena," Delly hollered.

Officer Tibbetts strode toward the girl. "Ferris Boyd!" she shouted, in that hard voice Delly'd heard a lot.

That didn't do it; the girl kept going.

Then, in a voice filled with kindness, Verena

called to her, "Ferris Boyd, look at me."

That did it. The girl stopped, and gazed into the policewoman's eyes.

"I will take care of you," she said surely.

They stared at each other for a long time, telling each other things without talking.

Finally, Officer Tibbetts nodded. She started toward the station, with Ferris Boyd beside her.

"We'll use the back door," she decided.

Inside, she pointed to a cell. "Go there."

She locked them in, and went to the front of the station. They sat on the bed.

"Hey, Ferris Boyd," Delly whispered, "they finally got me behind bars."

But her friend didn't hear her. Her right ear was up, listening to the other room.

"I found your daughter," Verena was saying.

There was mumbling.

"She can't go with you," the policewoman announced, "she's under arrest. She's staying with me for now."

There was muttering.

"You do what you have to do. I'll let you know if anything changes."

The front door thudded.

Then Officer Tibbetts was back. She had a big pad of paper and a pen. She set them beside Ferris Boyd. She squatted down in front of her, so their eyes were with each other. In that kind, sure voice, she said, "It's time to tell."

Chapter 72

That morning, when Brud Kinney'd gone to meet the bus, he found an old basketball sitting on his stoop. A small piece of paper was taped to it. BRUD, it read.

"H-h-hey." He grinned. He looked around for her, like she might be there to play; but it was only the ball.

Maybe she got a new one, he thought. Or maybe she thinks I'm good enough to have hers. He smiled so his teeth sparkled. With this ball, his head said, I'll play like nothing nobody's ever seen, only better.

In his hands, though, the ball didn't feel like a present. It felt like a good-bye.

When the bus stopped at Kinneys's, there was no Brud waiting, so it went on without him.

Brud Kinney was skipping school. He'd snuck out to the old Hennepin place, and was hiding in the bushes.

He'd never seen the green Impala before. So instead of going to the door, he walked to the drive and bounced the ball, ping, ping, ping, like a call.

Ferris Boyd didn't answer, but a man did. He stood at the door. "What do you want?" he hollered.

Brud dashed down the drive and out the River Road a ways. Then he circled back. He hid in the brush beside the drive.

He saw the police cruiser pull up. He spotted those copper curls in the passenger seat, but he didn't make a sound: He knew Verena was the truant officer, too.

Brud stayed till the cruiser took off. Then he snuck into River Bluffs.

From behind bushes, he watched Delly and Officer Tibbetts go to the river. A lot later, he saw them come back. With Ferris Boyd.

When his watch said the school day was over, Brud walked into the station.

Officer Tibbetts was at her desk doing paperwork. "What's up Brud?" she asked.

"Is Ferris B-B-Boyd here?"

"She's in the back," Verena answered.

"Can I s-s-s-see her?

"Sorry Brud. No visitors."

Brud stood there for a minute. Then he told her, "I stole this b-ball."

Verena glanced at it. "Brud," she told him, "nobody would steal that ball."

So Brud confessed, "I skipped school."

The policewoman studied him. "Brud," she wondered, "do you want me to arrest you?"

He nodded.

So she took him to the back.

As soon as she opened the door, there was a shout, "Hey, it's Brud Kinney!"

Then the station sounded more like a party than a prison.

Chapter 73

It was late when Officer Tibbetts brought Delly home. RB was waiting at the window.

"Is Ferris Boyd okay?" he whispered as they walked in, but Clarice cut him off.

"What's going on, Verena?" she demanded.

The policewoman started to explain how Delly'd come with her to find Ferris Boyd and bring her back from Delaferbia.

"What is Delaferbia?" Clarice exclaimed. "And who is Ferris Boyd?"

Officer Tibbetts had to get back to the station, so she turned to Delly.

"I'll tell her," Delly promised.

The policewoman went to the door. Before she left, though, she said, "Clarice, I'm not saying it's right to hide things. But we had a girl getting hurt, and now she's safe because of your daughter. That's something to keep in mind." And she was gone.

Clarice turned to Delly. "Speak," she commanded.

"Ferris Boyd is my friend." She began.

"Our friend," RB added.

Then she told Clarice how she met Ferris Boyd, how the project was really the hideawaysis, how they'd found Delaferbia. She told her about the green Impala and Ferris Boyd's father, about her running away and them bringing her back.

At first her mom was quiet, and Delly thought that was a good thing.

Till Clarice blew, like a nuclear bomb. "Every day...," she hollered, "sneaking...you might have... that man could have..."

She was putting things together, but not the way Delly wanted. "Not every day, Ma," she corrected her.

That put Clarice over the top. Her eyes got so big Delly thought they'd pop. She was just spitting sounds, "Puh...Heh... Ayhhh."

Suddenly, it stopped. They watched her, hoping the worst was over.

It wasn't. "I thought we were done with trouble," she hissed, "but this is the worst yet."

"Galveston," she shouted upstairs, "you are grounded for a year!"

"You, too." She pointed at RB.

"And you." She turned to Delly. "You are grounded for life."

"Go!" she ordered, directing them to the stairs.

So they did.

They sat on Delly's bed. "That's a long time." RB started crying, because he'd never been grounded before.

Delly put her arm around him. "It's okay," she told him, and it was. "Ferris Boyd's safe."

Chapter 74

That night, Delly went to Clarice, not because she was scared or couldn't sleep. She went because she wanted her mom to know something, right then and forever. She stood by the side of the bed. "Ma," she rasped.

"Delly," Clarice growled.

She bent down so she could feel the warmth of Clarice's cheek on her own. "Ma," she said, "I'm sorry. No more secrets, I promise."

Clarice didn't make a sound, so Delly turned to go.

"Delly," Clarice called, "stop."

So she did.

Clarice pulled back the covers. "Get in."

Delly lay down beside her.

In the darkness, Clarice said, "It's so hard, thinking something terrible could have happened to you and RB, and I didn't know anything." Her voice cracked, and she stopped for a second. "But what's harder is that you didn't trust me. Did you think I wouldn't help her?"

There were so many answers for one question: That Ferris Boyd wouldn't have wanted Clarice's help, that grownups had been around the girl every day and none of them had fixed it. Delly told the truest one, "I didn't know."

Clarice winced with that. "Delly," she said, "I want you to know this: If somebody's getting hurt, I will help."

Delly didn't need to see Clarice's eyes to know she was true. "Okay, Ma," she answered.

They lay there, then, gazing into the darkness.

After a while, Clarice asked, "Where is she now?"

"She's at Teeter's. They take foster kids."

"Hmm," Clarice murmured.

Delly could tell her mom was thinking something through, so she stayed quiet.

After a long time, Clarice turned to her daughter. "Del, I don't know the rules, so I can't promise anything," she told her. "But I'll talk to Verena tomorrow, and we'll see what we can do for your friend."

Then Delly didn't smile or shout, "Happy Hallelujah!" It was all too small for how she was feeling. "Ma," she whispered.

She put one arm across her mother's chest, and pulled till they were tight together. And Delly was a tiny love shield, her warm softness all around Clarice so nothing bad could get to her.

"Good night," she breathed. Because it was.

Dellyictionary

a dictionary of words invented by Delaware (Delly) Pattison

baDellyloon—Delly, so blown up with happiness she feels like a giant balloon.

Badkidville—a town for bad children, where Delly is afraid she'll end up.

Bawlgram—nocuss word used to describe a person, place, or thing that is offensive or irritating; e.g. the bawlgram cat.

Bawlgrammit—nocuss word, used to express anger, disgust, or frustration.

Bawldoublegrammit—"Bawlgrammit" times two.

Bugbotherer—someone who bugs and bothers others; a nuisance.

Chizzle—nocuss word, generally used when expressing anger, disappointment or disgust; the worst of the nocuss words.

Chizzlehead—someone with a head made of chizzle; the nastiest name for another person.

Delaferbia—a hideawaysis discovered by Delaware Pattison and named for its earliest explorers: Delly, Ferris, and RB.

Dellybrate—to celebrate in a Delly sort of way, often involving doughnuts, a trip to the river, and trouble.

Dellydebris—the debris that remains after an explosion of Delly's fury, e.g. tiny nuggets of what used to be Danny Novello

Dellyifferent—different than Delly; Delly transformed into somebody better.

Dellylicious—superlatively scrumptious; reserved for describing food of the utmost deliciousness, like triple chocolate doughnuts.

Dellymergency—an emergency of the most dire and extreme sort, as determined by Delly.

Dellypresents—a gift that Delly desires and gives to herself (as opposed to a surpresent, for which she would have to wait).

Dellypunishments—the varied assortment of punishments Delly has received over the years, ranging from brief detentions at school to being grounded for life.

Dellyventure—an adventure of the best sort, featuring Delly Pattison.

Fantabulous—fantastically fabulous

Fortrastle—a hideawaysis that has the protective qualities of a fortress and the regal appearance of a castle.

Getgorlying—getting going early.

Gimongous—humongously gigantic.

Glub (as in "What the glub?")—nocuss word, used to express dismay, shock, or frustration.

Happy Hallelujah—exclamation of maximum happiness.

Hideawaysis—a special, secret place, away from the rest of the world.

holiDelly—a holiday declared and celebrated by Delly, and only Delly.

Horribadible—horrible, terrible bad.

Hummin Bin—similar to a human being, but better. Hummin bins are kind, creative, gentle and good.

Idierk—an extremely obnoxious and ignorant person, e.g. Danny Novello.

Jiminy fipes—nocuss phrase, usually used as an expression of happiness, but can also indicate mild frustration or surprise.

Lugdraggerer—somebody who slows you down, and has to tie his shoe fifty times a day, e.g. RB Pattison.

Mistaster—a disastrous mistake.

Mysturiosity—a mystery that inspires curiosity, e.g. the sublimation of Ferris Boyd and Mowr.

Nocussictionary—a dictionary of words that replace cuss words. Using these words cannot get you in trouble.

Perfecterrific—something that's so terrific it seems perfect.

Perfexcellent—perfectly, precisely, profoundly excellent (perhaps).

reDellyformatory—a school that specializes in the betterment of bad children; a reformatory for Delly.

Shikes—nocuss word, used when expressing surprise, frustration, or anger.

Special Dellylivery—the delivery of Delly to her home by a person of authority, usually a police officer or school official, following the commission of a misdeed or crime.

Spitzooka—the mouth, utilized in such a manner that it becomes a bazooka for spit.

Surpresent—a present that's a surprise; the best kind of present possible.

Troubletale—a story of poor decisions and mistaken deeds, in which the protagonist (Delly) always ends up in the deep end of a pool of trouble.